"You feel so good in my arms."

He ran hot kisses across her cheek to her ear. "Don't go. Stay the night."

Her heart took a sudden dive. "You know I can't."

"You know you want to." His words sent splinters of ice dancing along her spine.

"Oh, Drew. You know me so well. Too well. It would be so simple to fall back into something that had been so…easy."

"Not to mention so good between us."

"We were good, Drew. But we said our goodbyes and moved on."

He shook his head. "We didn't move on. We just moved apart."

"Either way, it would be a mistake to let ourselves slip back, just for the sake of old times."

"Is that what you think? That what we felt just now was nostalgia?"

Dear Reader,

You've loved Beverly Barton's miniseries THE PROTECTORS since it started, so I know you'll be thrilled to find another installment leading off this month. *Navajo's Woman* features a to-swoon-for Native American hero, a heroine capable of standing up to this tough cop—and enough steam to heat your house. Enjoy!

A YEAR OF LOVING DANGEROUSLY continues with bestselling author Linda Turner's *The Enemy's Daughter.* This story of subterfuge and irresistible passion—not to mention heart-stopping suspense—is set in the Australian outback, and I know you'll want to go along for the ride. Ruth Langan completes her trilogy with *Seducing Celeste,* the last of THE SULLIVAN SISTERS. Don't miss this emotional read. Then check out Karen Templeton's *Runaway Bridesmaid,* a reunion romance with a heroine who's got quite a secret. Elane Osborn's *Which Twin?* offers a new twist on the popular twins plotline, while Linda Winstead Jones rounds out the month with *Madigan's Wife,* a wonderful tale of an ex-couple who truly belong together.

As always, we've got six exciting romances to tempt you—and we'll be back next month with six more. Enjoy!

Leslie J. Wainger
Executive Senior Editor

Please address questions and book requests to:
Silhouette Reader Service
U.S.: 3010 Walden Ave., P.O. Box 1325, Buffalo, NY 14269
Canadian: P.O. Box 609, Fort Erie, Ont. L2A 5X3

Seducing Celeste
RUTH LANGAN

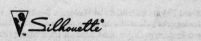

INTIMATE MOMENTS™

Published by Silhouette Books

America's Publisher of Contemporary Romance

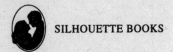 SILHOUETTE BOOKS

ISBN 0-373-27135-2

SEDUCING CELESTE

Copyright © 2001 by Ruth Ryan Langan

This edition published by arrangement with Harlequin Books S.A.

® and TM are trademarks of Harlequin Books S.A., used under license.
Trademarks indicated with ® are registered in the United States Patent
and Trademark Office, the Canadian Trade Marks Office and in other
countries.

Visit Silhouette at www.eHarlequin.com

Printed in U.S.A.

RUTH LANGAN

Award-winning and bestselling author Ruth Langan creates characters that *Affaire de Coeur* magazine has called "so incredibly human the reader will expect them to come over for tea." Four of Ruth's books have been finalists for the Romance Writers of America's (RWA) RITA Award. Over the years, she has given dozens of print, radio and TV interviews, including some for *Good Morning America* and *CNN News,* and has been quoted in such diverse publications as the *The Wall Street Journal, Cosmopolitan* and *The Detroit Free Press.* Married to her childhood sweetheart, she has raised five children and lives in Michigan, the state where she was born and raised.

For Ryan Paul Langan, a very special gift to his parents, Mike and Patty, and his sisters, Kelly and Riley.

For his grandfather, Paul Cornish, guardian angel and one of heaven's brightest lights.

And for his other grandfather, Tom Langan, who owns my heart.

Prologue

Paris, 1979

"Grandpa Sully. Grandpa Sully." Three little girls eagerly flung themselves into the arms of the handsome, ruddy Irishman as soon as he stepped into the courtyard of the Paris hotel.

Patrick Joseph Sullivan, patriarch of the Sullivan clan, was called Paddy by his friends, and Grandpa Sully by his adored granddaughters.

"Oh, how I've missed this. Missed the three of you." He scooped them up one by one, loving the feel of chubby arms around his neck and wet, sloppy kisses on his mouth.

"Look what I made you, Grandpa Sully." Alex,

the oldest, and an avowed tomboy, handed him a
bird's nest she'd found beneath a tree.

"Well, isn't this grand." He knelt beside her
and accepted her gift with all the delight of a boy
on his birthday. "And what's this inside?"

"Eggshell. One of the baby birds left his shell
behind when he flew away. See? It's speckled."
She held up the fragments for his inspection.

"I see."

"Next year, if we're still here, I'm going to
climb up the tree and visit the babies before they're
old enough to fly."

"We won't be here next year." Celeste, the
youngest of the three, with red hair and enormous
green eyes, spoke with an air of authority.

"And why won't you?" her grandfather asked.

"Because Mama says hotel people don't live
anywhere for more than a year."

"Right you are, my little darlin'. And why is
that?"

"Because there's always a new hotel needing
our help."

"Right again." He turned to his middle granddaughter. "What's this? A gift for me?"

Lizbeth dimpled. "It's called a scone. Cook let
me help her in the kitchen this morning. I baked
this just for you, Grandpa Sully."

He took a bite and gave a hum of pleasure.
"Now that was worth flying all the way from Ven-

ice, Lizzybeth. I hope you'll make me more before I leave.''

"I'm going to make you fifty jillion, Grandpa Sully." Delighted at the success of her gift, the little girl danced away to pester the hotel cook for more lessons.

The old man turned to his youngest granddaughter, so serious, so solemn, who had patiently waited her turn, holding her gift behind her back.

"Do you have something for me, darlin' lass?''

She nodded and lifted her hand to reveal a lovely pen and ink drawing of a weathered New England building.

Patrick Sullivan studied it with a look of admiration. "Did you draw this freehand, or did you trace it?''

"I drew it, Grandpa Sully. I heard you telling Mama and Papa that it was time for another hotel, and I thought this looked like a nice one."

"A nice one indeed. Where did you see it?''

"In a travel poster. It was in a place called New Hamster.''

He threw back his head and roared. "That's New Hampshire, lass. A pretty state in the eastern United States.''

"Have you been there, Grandpa?''

"Indeed I have. That's where my hunting lodge is. Maybe I'll take you there next summer. Would you like that?''

The little girl nodded, and for the first time her smile came, bright enough to rival the sun. "Maybe some day I'll live in a hotel in New Hamst...New Hampshire."

Her grandfather gave her a quick hug. "If you do, lass, I'll expect it to be the most profitable hotel in our chain."

"It will be, Grandpa Sully."

"That's my girl." He caught her hand and started inside the elegant Paris hotel that the children and their parents currently called home.

It occurred to Paddy Sullivan that of his three granddaughters, this one was the most like him. Driven to be the best at whatever she chose to do. She seemed to not only adapt to change, but to thrive on it. She loved mastering the language and learning the customs of every country in which she lived. And her exposure to art, music and style throughout the world had already given her a cosmopolitan air unusual in one so young.

Oh, this one was a Sullivan, through and through.

He had no doubt that his darlin' Celeste would succeed at whatever she set her mind to.

Chapter 1

Liberty, New Hampshire

"Good morning, Miss Celeste." The old man holding open the elevator door of the Old Liberty Tavern looked as weathered as the building he guarded so zealously. But, despite the lines etched deeply into his face, and the thatch of white hair, there was a perpetual twinkle in his blue eyes. He stood ramrod straight, the crease in his trousers perfectly pressed, the tip of a crisp handkerchief peeking from the breast pocket of his navy jacket.

Jeremiah Cross was a fixture at the Old Liberty Tavern, starting work as a dishwasher when he'd been so small he'd had to stand on a stool to reach the sink. He could still remember a time where there had been a barn behind the building for the travelers' horses. Now he greeted guests, held doors and did whatever needed doing, all with warmth and wry New England charm.

"Good morning, Jeremiah." Celeste Sullivan gave him a bright smile. She couldn't decide whether it had been this man, one of her grandfather's closest friends, or the location that had first won her heart. A year in this picturesque setting wasn't nearly enough. The old Yankee town of Liberty was New England to its core. It could have easily been used on travel posters, nestled as it was between the massive slopes of the White Mountains and bounded by pristine lakes and woods of towering pine. There was even a covered bridge and an ancient mill still operating beside a sparkling pond.

"The weatherman says it's going to be a perfect summer day."

He smiled. "Yes, indeed. A good thing, too. The Rotary Club plans on holding its monthly luncheon in the courtyard."

"Thanks for reminding me, Jeremiah." She swept past him into the foyer, calling over her shoulder, "I'll be sure to put in an appearance."

"They'll appreciate that, my dear."

Bitsy Hillerman, home from college for the summer, stood at the reception area talking on the phone. Her name was actually Betsy, but because of her tiny stature she'd been dubbed Bitsy by the other employees. She looked up and waved as her boss breezed past. Celeste returned the salute before disappearing inside her office.

"'Morning, Ms. Sullivan." Celeste's new assistant-in-training, Daniel O'Malley, got to his feet and reached over the desk to hand her a bundle of papers. Recently arrived from the Sullivan-owned Castle Dunniefey in Ireland, his brogue was thick enough to cut.

"Your mail. And a list of today's activities. There's to be a luncheon in the courtyard at noon."

Celeste nodded. "The Rotary Club. What else?"

He scanned the list. "The B.M.C. Corporation is scheduled for the main dining room. A business lunch and motivational speaker. They're scheduled to end at five. There's a wine-tasting, sponsored by the local restaurants to benefit the Liberty Children's Hospital, from six-thirty to eight, followed by Dinner Under The Stars in the courtyard. And the Liberty High School is taking over the ballroom tonight for their prom."

When he paused to take a breath, Celeste gave a smile of satisfaction. "Well, Daniel, I'd say that's a pretty fair Friday."

So much for the fear that the Old Liberty Tavern was doomed for the wrecking ball. She'd been here less than a year and already the profits were through the roof. Of course, she'd had to give up any thought of a social life to achieve her goal. And she'd moved from a nearby cottage on the grounds to a top-floor suite so that she could be closer to her work. Work which often ran to eighteen- and twenty-hour days.

Still, she thought as she turned toward her inner office, success was the sweetest revenge.

With her hand on the knob, Daniel said, "If you could wait a bit, Ms. Sullivan."

She glanced over her shoulder.

"There's someone in there to see you."

"Really? Who?"

"A representative from Van Dorn Hotels." Daniel picked up a business card from his desk. "Mr. Andrew Hampton."

Celeste's smile faded as she accepted the card from his hand. She stared at the name as though unable to believe what she was reading. Then she leaned a hand on the back of a chair to steady herself as she read his title. Executive vice-president.

He'd wasted no time.

It took her only an instant to compose herself. By the time she turned toward her door, there was no sign of the nerves simmering just below the surface.

She opened the door and stepped into her inner office, smoothly switching the papers to her left hand so that she could offer a handshake to the man who got quickly to his feet.

"Hello, Drew."

"Celeste."

She kept the contact brisk, impersonal. If she felt a sizzle of heat along her arm, she ignored it as she stepped around her desk and took a seat.

Her visitor did the same, waiting until she was seated to settle himself in the chair, crossing his legs at the ankles in a relaxed manner. She wondered if it was all a pose. The Drew Hampton she'd known was about as relaxed as a panther coiled on a high perch, about to strike any unsuspecting prey foolish enough to let down its guard.

Celeste was grateful for the desk between them. But it wasn't nearly enough of a barrier to protect her from the almost palpable energy that seemed to radiate from this man.

How was it possible for him to look even better than she remembered? Tall. Tan. Fit. His dark hair cut razor short. Those gray eyes full of shadow and mystery. His lips, those incredible lips, smiling at her in a way that always managed to tug at her heart.

"What brings you to the States, Drew? I thought you'd found a home on the French Riviera. Or was it London?"

"London. But the powers-that-be at Van Dorn

Hotels decided they wanted to turn my talents in another direction.''

She glanced at his business card, then tossed it aside. "I see you've climbed the corporate ladder.''

He nodded. "I'm in purchasing."

"As in supplies?''

He heard the hint of sarcasm. His smile was slow and lazy. "Hotel sites. We're looking to expand across the country."

"What are you doing in Liberty? Isn't this just a little off the beaten track?''

"Not at all. In fact, it's come to our attention that, after charting its profits for the past year, this historic old inn has become a prime piece of property.''

Even while she absorbed the pleasure of knowing that her success was being followed by the competition, she felt a quick sting of annoyance. "Sorry. It's not for sale.''

"That's not what your grandfather hinted.''

She stiffened. Her voice took on an edge of anger. "You talked to Grandpa Sully about this?''

"He's still chairman of the board of Sullivan Hotels, isn't he?''

"Yes, but…''

Drew held up a hand. "I don't want you to think I was going behind your back, Celeste. But you know how these things work. Van Dorn stated their intention. Sullivan Hotels invited us to observe the operation and look over the books, before making an offer to purchase.''

Her hands closed around the edge of the desk, gripping so tightly her knuckles whitened. ''Grandpa Sully gave you permission to…observe my operation?''

''He not only gave his permission…'' Drew shrugged. ''…he encouraged me to spend as much time as I wanted. I'd call that a friendly overture toward arriving at some sort of amicable arrangement that would suit both our companies.'' He gave her a measured look. ''I'm surprised he didn't call and let you know I'd be coming.''

Knowing her grandfather, he'd have called her private number rather than her business phone. Celeste thought about the telephone answering machine in her suite. Had she remembered to play it the last couple of nights? Not that she could recall. She'd put in so many hours, starting at dawn, finally collapsing into bed after midnight, she'd barely had time to wash off her makeup before it was time to get dressed again.

''He may have called.'' The way Drew was watching her made her yearn for somewhere to hide. He knew her well enough to see through her discomfort. ''I'm afraid I'll be too busy today to show you around. But if you'd like my assistant…''

He was already on his feet, his smile still in place. "That isn't necessary. I assure you, Celeste, I don't intend to get in your way. Just go about your business as though I'm not even here. I'll just tag along like your shadow." He started toward the door, then turned. "The young woman at the reservation desk, Bitsy, has already offered to see to my room. I'm afraid it will have to be an open-ended reservation, since I don't know how long I'll be here. No more than a day or two at most."

When he was gone Celeste sat staring at the closed door. She couldn't recall a single word she'd spoken. All she knew was that Drew Hampton had just walked back into her life. As casually, as callously, as he had once walked out. And all those feelings she'd worked so hard to bury had just come rushing back to taunt her.

She ought to hate him. Wanted to. But at the moment all she could think about was the way she'd felt when their hands had touched. The same jolt of electricity charging through her system with all the force of a lightning bolt. And the heat she'd experienced just looking at his mouth, remembering how it felt pressed to hers.

She shoved back her chair and got to her feet. What kind of a fool was she that she'd sit here and allow him to open up old wounds? Allow him to draw blood all over again? Drew Hampton had trampled on her heart in his haste to get to the top

of the corporate ladder. She was older now.
Smarter. And definitely tougher. She'd survived
the pain by immersing herself in her work. That
would be her salvation now. A day or two, he'd
said. Fine. For the next day or two she intended to
fill every hour of both day and night with hard,
satisfying work. And when he left her this time,
she'd have the satisfaction of telling him not to let
the door hit his backside on the way out.

Drew stood back watching as Celeste moved
among the tables in the courtyard, pausing to greet
every guest by name. They responded with smiles
and jokes and friendly remarks.

People had always been her strong suit. It was
a Sullivan gift, passed down from parent to child.
Maybe it was the Irish in them, he thought. The
Sullivan family had never met a stranger they
couldn't charm into becoming a friend.

That first sight of her had been quite a jolt. He'd
thought that he'd had plenty of time to prepare
himself during the long flight from London. But
nothing could prepare a man for a woman like Celeste Sullivan. He watched her with more than a
trace of admiration. She was quite a package. The
red hair was shorter now, chin length, tucked behind one ear. The green eyes may have been cool
when they met his, but he'd been reminded of the
way they could gleam like fire when she was

aroused. The pale green suit was Armani, quiet, elegant, understated. But it couldn't hide the killer body underneath. A body he'd once known as intimately as his own. Even her perfume had been the same as he'd remembered. A light floral fragrance that he could still smell in his dreams. He'd spent many a night waking in a sweat, his body yearning for hers, his lungs filled with the fragrance of wildflowers.

In the privacy of her office it had taken every ounce of self-control to keep from dragging her into his arms and covering those pouting lips with his. Even now, watching her as she talked and laughed easily with her guests, the mere sway of her hips had his throat going dry, his hands clenching into fists at his sides.

His cell phone rang. He snatched it from his inside pocket and answered it on the second ring. ''Drew Hampton.''

''Andrew.''

''Mr. Van Dorn.'' Drew's tone sharpened when he recognized the voice of the chairman of the board of Van Dorn Hotels. A man who'd made it abundantly clear when he'd hired Drew that he was already scouting a successor.

Like Patrick Sullivan, Eric Van Dorn had spent a lifetime owning and operating hotels. Though the two men were friendly rivals, their attitudes about life and business were very different. Patrick Sullivan's work was his life. Eric Van Dorn had a life apart from his work. A life that seemed to call to him more with each passing year.

"So. What do you think about the potential of our latest addition to the company?"

Drew knew he ought to be flattered that the chairman considered the deal already finalized. It was a tribute to his skill as a negotiator. But instead he felt a quick flash of annoyance. These things couldn't be decided on a whim and a glance. "It looks interesting. But hardly a done deal. I'll need some time to look around."

"Don't take too long, Andrew. I wouldn't want this fish to wiggle off the hook."

Drew winced. Everyone in the company knew how much the chairman loved fly-fishing. It was, in fact, the real love of his life. He yearned to retire and spend his days on a quiet wilderness lake, in pursuit of the legendary catch. Because of that fact his employees had learned to couch all their discussions in language that would appeal to him.

"Don't you worry, Mr. Van Dorn. As soon as I figure out the best lure, I'll reel it in for you."

"See that you do, Andrew. Van Dorn Hotels need all the big ones they can net. And these statistics on the Old Liberty Tavern are looking better all the time."

Drew disconnected and returned his phone to his

pocket. The sound of Celeste's laughter carried on the breeze.

What the hell had he been thinking, agreeing to come here to observe the operation? At the time it had seemed like a good idea. Now he was beginning to second-guess himself.

In today's competitive market there were plenty of hotels and inns that were going under, and could be bought for a bargain. This wasn't the only one his company had an interest in. But the fact that it was showing such a marked profit when, just a year ago it was failing, had moved it to the top of the company's wish list.

When Drew had realized that Celeste was the one responsible for its success, he'd been instantly attracted. And when the board of directors asked him to handle this fact-finding mission, he'd been more than ready.

Now they'd expect a miracle. And, he thought watching Celeste shaking hands with the officers of the Rotary Club, that's probably what it would take for him to make a deal here.

He might be able to persuade the board of Sullivan Hotels to sell at a profit. After all, a year ago they'd been ready to bail out of a sinking ship. But that was before Celeste had stepped in and pumped up the business. He'd seen the way she'd looked when she'd learned that her grandfather had already approved the first step in this buy-out. It had been more than professional competitiveness that had flared darkly in her eyes. She'd been personally offended. And more wounded than she'd wanted to let on.

With Celeste, he realized, this wasn't just about business. Knowing how she operated, he'd be willing to bet that she'd been pouring her heart and soul into this operation. Eating and sleeping cost-control and profit-and-loss figures. She'd probably put her life on hold just to make this place a success. And now, he was threatening to buy it out from under her.

No, he thought. With Celeste, it wasn't about business. Especially now that she'd met the competition. Seeing him here had made it much more personal.

But then, hadn't it been the same for him? The minute he'd seen her name in the financial records, he'd known that this was where he wanted to be.

He stopped beside a lovely fountain and, with his hands linked behind his back, stared down into the falling water as though searching for something in its depths. It was time for a little honesty. Though he may have fooled himself into thinking so in the beginning, it was no longer honest to suggest, even to himself, that he was merely here on business. He'd come to Liberty for something much deeper. Something infinitely more important than making another score in the world of hotel finance.

He and Celeste had parted badly. His fault, he knew. That knowledge still rubbed his heart raw. He intended to use this opportunity to finish what they'd started a long time ago.

One way or another.

Chapter 2

"Ms. Sullivan."

Celeste held the cell phone to her ear as she continued across the courtyard. "Yes, Daniel." She smiled at several of her employees while she listened attentively to the voice of her assistant.

"You asked me to let you know when the representative from the linen service arrived. He's here in your office."

"Thanks, Daniel. I'll be right there." She tucked the phone into her pocket and started toward the executive offices, pausing now and then to speak to the wait staff cleaning up from the noon luncheon.

All morning she'd been achingly aware of Drew

dogging her footsteps. Like a shadow, he'd said.
But it felt more like a burr. One that stuck to her
skin. Not enough to be painful, but just enough to
be exceedingly uncomfortable.

It had been a struggle to ignore the prickling
along her spine that signaled his presence directly
behind her. But it had spurred her on to lose herself
even more completely in her work. In the four
hours since she'd left her office, she hadn't once
paused for breath.

But that didn't mean that she had managed to
forget him for even a moment.

When she passed the front desk she saw Jeremiah Cross assisting an elderly woman with her
luggage. She felt a flash of alarm. At his age, such
work could be dangerous. Still, she knew better
than to suggest such a thing to him. Instead she
stepped behind the desk and peered into the back
room, where two college students, working as bellmen for the summer, were on their lunch break.

The taller of the two looked up. "Did you need
something, Ms. Sullivan?"

She nodded and said quietly, "Jeremiah needs
some help."

The two set aside their sandwiches and sodas
and hurried out front to lend a hand. As Celeste
continued on toward her office, she saw with satisfaction that the young men were hauling the suit-

cases, while Jeremiah was free to escort their guest into the elevator.

Behind her Drew merely smiled. Leave it to Celeste to handle delicate matters with diplomacy. The old man wouldn't even notice that she'd intervened.

She stepped into her office and Daniel got to his feet. "I asked the gentleman from the linen service to wait in your office. His name is Frank Cormeyer."

"Thank you, Daniel. Will you take a message to our young bellmen, please. From now on, I want one of them on duty at all times. They're not to take their breaks together."

She said this in the same conversational tone she always used. And yet her assistant noted the thread of steel beneath the words.

He nodded. "I'll see to it right away."

Celeste opened the door to her inner office and stepped inside. And though it would have given her immense pleasure to close the door in Drew's face, she knew she had to honor her grandfather's word and permit him entry into every phase of her operation.

"Mr. Cormeyer?" She watched as a burly man with graying hair and the face of a boxer, with a flattened nose and a long, thin scar beneath his left eye, lumbered to his feet and towered over her.

"That's right." He looked from her to the man

who entered behind her. "I was told to wait in here to meet with the boss. I guess that'd be you."

Drew shook his head. "You'd guess wrong. I'm just a visitor. Ms. Sullivan is the boss here."

"Celeste Sullivan." She offered her hand.

The man swallowed back his surprise and returned her handshake.

"Now, Mr. Cormeyer." She rounded the desk and sat facing him. "We signed a contract with your company in good faith. You promised to deliver clean linen to our inn between the hours of nine and eleven every day except Sunday."

He nodded. "I explained to the head of your housekeeping department. Our trucks had a few breakdowns."

"A few? In the last thirty days, your truck has been late seventeen times. That's seventeen days that our household staff was late making up rooms for incoming guests."

"Look. We supply a lot of businesses. You act like you're the only one we have to worry about." He shrugged. "What's a couple of hours here and there?"

"I'll tell you what a couple of hours mean to a business like ours, Mr. Cormeyer. First and foremost, unhappy guests who won't choose to stay at the Old Liberty Tavern next time they're in town, because when they checked in, they found the bed unmade, the bath linens soiled. And then there's the matter of overtime for the household staff forced to stay late in order to finish their chores. Every time your linen service is late, you're costing me time and money.''

"I'll talk to our drivers.''

She steepled her hands and studied him across the desk. "That would be wise, Mr. Cormeyer. You see I spoke with our legal firm this morning and they have informed your company in writing that one more late delivery will find you in violation of your contract. It will result in immediate termination.''

He leaned forward, wearing a scowl guaranteed to freeze the heart of anyone foolish enough to oppose him. "Look, missy. Don't try cutting off your nose to spite your face. If you terminate our contract, what'll you do for linen for this place?''

She kept her tone even, her smile in place. "I met with two of your competitors yesterday. Both of them agreed to meet or beat your price, and gave me a guarantee of early-morning delivery.'' She glanced at her watch. "You might want to wait at the rear loading dock for your driver. He's now overdue by more than two hours. I left word with my housekeeping staff not to accept delivery until you had a chance to speak with him.''

The man's face was suffused with color as he shuffled to his feet. If he'd thought to frighten this small, elegant female with his back-alley manners, she'd called his bluff. "I'll speak with him. He won't be late again."

She stood as well. "Thank you, Mr. Cormeyer. I appreciate that."

When the door closed behind him, Drew saw the way she took in one long, slow breath before sinking back down to her chair.

He felt a wave of admiration for the way in which she'd handled the situation.

Without a word he let himself out of her office, allowing her some much-deserved privacy.

"Thanks, Daniel." Celeste handed her assistant a pile of documents bearing her signature. "I think that's the last of the correspondence. At least for now."

As he was walking out of her office, Drew appeared, carrying a linen-covered tray.

She looked up in annoyance. "What's this?"

"Lunch." He set it in the center of her desk and lifted the linen napkin to reveal a large salad and a basket of crusty dinner rolls, accompanied by a pot of tea and two cups. "I spoke with your cook, Marcus, and he said you haven't taken time for breakfast or lunch in weeks."

"How would he know? Maybe I eat in the privacy of my room."

"Yeah. And maybe you're cooking on a hot plate. We both know how much you love cooking for yourself.'' He grinned and began arranging the salad in two crystal bowls. Then he drew a chair beside hers and handed her a cruet of olive oil and red wine vinegar.

She stared down at the salad of tomatoes and onions drizzled with Gorgonzola cheese. "I haven't tasted this since..."

"Rome," he finished for her.

"That's right. That little inn." She saw him looking at her and ducked her head. But after one bite, she couldn't hide her pleasure. "Oh, this is wonderful. I didn't know Marcus even had this recipe."

"He didn't. I made it."

"You did?" She took another bite before breaking a roll and handing him half.

Their fingers brushed. This time, instead of being annoyed, she found the rush of heat pleasantly soothing. Like a half-remembered dream.

It wasn't that she was softening her attitude about Drew. It was merely the presence of food. And not just any food.

"I didn't know you liked to cook."

"One of my many newly acquired talents. It was either that, or starve when I found myself in a little out-of-the-way inn with no room service." He dipped the roll into a mixture of olive oil and vinegar, with a sprinkling of parmesan cheese, and held it to her mouth.

She had no choice but to taste. This time, when his fingers brushed her lips, the heat was stronger, the feelings much more than merely pleasant. She struggled to push them aside.

"Umm. That's delicious. Where did you find this?"

"I first tasted it on a little Mediterranean island." He leaned close and lowered his voice to a whisper. "If you'd like, I'll trust your cook with the secret ingredients."

She couldn't help laughing. "That's the same thing the cook in that little inn in Rome said to you."

He smiled, pleased that she hadn't forgotten. "No. What he said was he'd trust me with the recipe because I was with the most beautiful woman who had ever graced his dining room. If you recall, he kissed his fingers to his lips and called you sheer perfection."

Remembering, Celeste blushed. "And then he brought us a bottle of his best wine and asked if we would share it with him."

"I don't think he cared whether or not I drank any." Drew chuckled. "In fact, he was hoping I'd get lost so he could have you all to himself."

"Not at all, Drew. Don't you remember?" She touched a hand to his arm, then just as quickly withdrew it. But not before she saw his eyes narrow slightly. "He…" She fought to keep her voice steady. "He enjoyed your company. What's more, he shared his secret recipe with you. And you have to admit he was a terrific cook."

"Yes, he was." Drew poured tea and placed a steaming cup in front of her. "He was also a shameless flirt."

Celeste looked down and was surprised to see that she'd finished every bite of her salad and roll. As she sipped her tea it occurred to her that she felt better than she had in hours.

Drew had always had a sixth sense about her, knowing when she needed a break to eat, to rest, to marshal her energy for the job at hand. It had been one of the things she'd loved about being with him. After they'd gone their separate ways, she'd missed that more than she'd cared to admit.

When her phone rang, she reluctantly turned away to answer it. "Yes, Daniel. That's fine. I'll take his call. And tell legal to fax those documents. I'll get back with them as soon as I've had time to read through them."

She looked up. "Thanks, Drew. That was really nice. But I'm afraid this can't wait."

"No problem."

She sighed and watched as Drew set the remains of their lunch on the tray and quietly let himself out of her office.

It had been a pleasant interlude. But now it was time to get back to reality.

* * *

"Just look at them." Jeremiah Cross stood outside the double doors of the ballroom and watched the parade of high school seniors. The girls floated by in their pastel prom gowns, while the boys made every attempt to look casual in their rented tuxedos. "I don't believe I was ever that young."

Celeste patted his arm. "I was just thinking the same thing."

"You?" He swiveled his head to look her in the eye. "You're in the prime of your life. Why, when I was your age, I had the feeling that the whole world was mine for the taking."

"And did you take it, Jeremiah?"

He winked. "You bet I did. With both hands." He pointed at the throng of students dancing. "But I never went to one of these."

"Neither did I."

At her admission he turned to her. "What's that supposed to mean?"

"It means that the senior prom is strictly an American tradition. They didn't offer it in the Swiss boarding school I attended."

"Well then, we're going to have to do something about that little omission from your youth." The old man made a grand bow. "Miss Celeste Sullivan, may I have this dance?"

It was on the tip of her tongue to refuse. She'd already lingered here long enough. She had at least a dozen more things to see to before the evening ended. But he looked so sweet, his gnarled old hands reaching out to hers.

With a laugh she nodded. "Jeremiah, I thought you'd never ask."

Fortunately the music was something soft and slow. Not that it would have mattered. Jeremiah Cross appeared to be a man who moved to his own music. He swept her into a graceful waltz, and they moved along the fringes of the dancers.

Celeste looked up into twinkling blue eyes. "Jeremiah, you're a wonderful dancer."

"Thank you."

She shot him a speculative look. "You're too smooth to be a rookie. Have you been holding out on me? I know we've never talked about this before, but were you a professional dancer in your youth?"

"I did a little of it."

"A little? You did more than a little. Where did you do this dancing?"

"On Broadway. During one of those many breaks to restore my spirit."

"Oh, be still my heart. I'm dancing with a professional dancer."

"On Broadway we called ourselves hoofers."

She gave a laugh as he twirled her and spun her, all the while deftly moving her around the floor until they arrived back where they'd started.

As the music ended he released her, then made a graceful bow. "Thank you for letting an old man remember his youth."

"And thank you, Jeremiah, for my first prom dance."

He lifted her hand to his lips, then turned. "Good evening, Mr. Hampton."

"Jeremiah." Drew kept his gaze on Celeste. "What did you mean by your first prom?"

"I was telling Jeremiah that it's an American custom. They didn't have proms at my boarding school."

"That's a shame. You missed something special."

"Exactly what I was telling her." The old man stepped aside and neatly pushed the two together. "Show her what she missed, Mr. Hampton."

Drew felt the brush of her body against his and smiled as his arms came around her. "Care to dance?"

"No, I..."

It was too late. He was already moving her slowly to the music. She held herself stiffly, trying not to feel his hand at her back, or the way his breath skimmed her cheek. Or the brush of his body against hers.

"I suppose you went to a lot of proms." She looked up at him, then away, hoping he couldn't feel the way her heart had suddenly gone into spasm.

"One. My senior year. It set me back so much money, I had to work overtime for a month. But it was worth it. I took Rosemary Tucci. She was considered the babe of the class. Big brown eyes. Big hair. Big..." He shrugged. Grinned. And was glad to see that she was laughing.

"It bought me a lot of bragging rights."

"I suppose that's important to a guy." She struggled to ignore the heat of his touch, but it was impossible.

"Everything's important to a guy when he's young and restless and his testosterone is raging."

"I thought that was a condition of men until they were a hundred and five."

He threw back his head and laughed. "Guilty, ma'am."

Celeste was grateful when the music ended. This was much too uncomfortable.

As they stepped apart, she saw Jeremiah looking unusually pleased with himself. He was such an old dear. He probably thought his little attempt to get her a dance partner more her age was nothing more than a harmless distraction. He couldn't possibly know what it did to her heart.

"Well." She kept her tone light. "Now I see what I missed."

Drew nodded toward the courtyard, aglow with

hurricane candles. "You also missed the wine-tasting. Want to get some dinner?"

Just then her cell phone rang. As she retrieved it from her pocket she shook her head. "Sorry. My day's not over yet. But you go ahead."

When she walked away Drew folded his arms over his chest and watched in silence. He needed to beware what he asked for. He'd come here hoping she hadn't changed too much. That much had been given him. But it would seem that her attitude about work hadn't changed either. She still thought she could outsmart time and work around the clock without paying a price.

What she needed, what she'd always needed, was somebody to see to all the little details of living, while she was busy working.

What she needed, he thought with a frown, was a keeper.

He looked up to see Jeremiah watching him. With a wave of his hand he strode away.

Celeste glanced at the ancient clock in the entrance foyer. Two-thirty in the morning, and she'd been on her feet since early the previous morning. She smiled at the sleepy night clerk manning the front desk as she made her way to the elevator.

Just as she stepped inside and punched the button to the top floor, she heard a footstep and looked up to see Drew stepping in beside her.

"Aren't you keeping awfully late hours?"

His smile was quick. "I might say the same for you. Is this a typical day?"

She sighed. "It seems to be a trend lately." She glanced over. "What floor are you on?"

"The top floor."

Her smile vanished. "And how did that happen? Did you request it?"

"As a matter of fact, your reservation clerk, Bitsy, assigned it. If that's a problem for you, I could ask her to change it."

"No. Of course not." Celeste dismissed the quick flutter of nerves as simple exhaustion. He couldn't possibly have known where she was staying. Could he?

When they reached the top, the doors glided silently open and Drew waited for her to step out first. They padded along the hallway carpeted in rich burgundy, dimly lit by ancient copper sconces outfitted with bulbs that flickered like candles.

She paused outside the door of her suite. After withdrawing the key from her pocket and unlocking the door, she turned. "I must say, I never dreamed when I left my room this morning that I'd be saying good-night to you, Drew."

He gave her a lazy smile and took a step closer, enjoying the way she backed up. "You know what they say. What a difference a day makes."

She hesitated when she felt the cool wall behind

her. "I suppose you'll have to file a report before you turn in."

He shook his head. "Unlike you, Celeste, I'm not driven to cram twenty-five hours into every twenty-four."

"Really? Then you must have had an epiphany since you started working at Van Dorn. The Drew Hampton I knew used to love working around the clock."

He shrugged. "I'm willing to save something for another day. Tomorrow's soon enough."

"Then I hope tomorrow always comes for you."

He reached out and caught a strand of her hair, watching as the fiery strands sifted through his fingers. "I'm counting on it."

She fought the nerves that skittered along her spine. "Goodnight, Drew."

When she started to turn she felt his hand at her shoulder. She spun back, determined to put him in his place.

He recognized all the signs of temper. The fire in those green eyes, like points of flame. The flare of nostrils. The defiant lift of her chin. Her temper had always been wonderful to watch, like a display of brilliant fireworks.

"I'm so glad you haven't changed, Celeste."

"But I have changed. And, in case you haven't noticed, so have things between us. I don't want you touching me, Drew."

''Sorry. I have to. Just this once.'' His hands closed around her upper arms as he dragged her close and lowered his face to hers.

Reading his intention, her throat went dry, her eyes narrowed with disapproval.

He took no notice as his mouth covered hers.

At first the kiss was soft, hesitant. Celeste knew she ought to pull back, slap his face and lock herself away in her room where she would be safe. But it was already too late. The instant his mouth moved over hers, she was lost.

She stood very still, absorbing shockwave after shockwave, while the floor seemed to pitch and tilt, and her mind was wiped clean of every thought except one. He was the only man who had ever had the ability to affect her like this. His were the only lips that had ever made the earth move. And the hands moving along her shoulders, down her back, setting tiny fires along her spine, were the only ones capable of reducing her to whimpers of pure pleasure.

She hated that. It was a weakness in herself she despised. But there it was.

He'd known. The minute he'd seen her this morning, he'd known that all the feelings were still there between them. Or at least he'd hoped. And when he'd held her on the dance floor, it had all come flooding back to him. The heat. The fire. The need. Now, holding her, kissing her, all doubt was gone. Nothing had changed. He still wanted her.

He knew he had to stop. But he couldn't find the will. Not yet. Not when her lips were so sweet, and her sighs were filling his mouth with the honeyed taste he'd never been able to forget. Not when he was drunk on the perfume of wildflowers that filled his lungs.

He lingered over her lips a moment longer, drawing out the taste, the pleasure, until he could summon the strength to step back. It would be so easy to drag her inside and shut out the world. To take and take until they were both sated. It was what he wanted. All he wanted. And right now, hearing her sighs of pleasure, he had no doubt it was what she wanted, too. But it was all happening too fast. There were too many barriers between them now.

Calling on all his willpower he lifted his head. Keeping his hands on her shoulders he waited until his world settled.

He pressed his lips to a tangle of hair at her temple. "Goodnight, Celeste."

Without a word she turned and walked through the doorway, then closed the door firmly and threw the bolt.

She leaned her forehead against the closed door and listened to his muffled footsteps. When she

heard the door open and close across the hall, she
let out a long, deep sigh.

All those feelings she'd thought dead and buried
had suddenly come rushing back, catching her by
surprise. And all it had taken from Drew Hampton
was one kiss. One simple kiss to light the fire.

Simple? She touched a fingertip to her lips.
There had been nothing simple about that kiss. The
touch of him, the taste of him, were still there, as
powerful, as potent as ever.

She crossed the room and sank down on the
edge of the bed, feeling completely shattered.

Why had he walked back into her life now? Was
this about business? Or was there something else
going on?

Either way, she had to gather the courage to
keep him from getting to her. Otherwise she'd
never have any self-respect left when he was gone.

And he would be gone, she reminded herself. A
day or two at most, was all that would be needed
to observe the operation here and examine the
books. And then Drew Hampton would be gone
again. Blowing into and then out of her life like a
fierce summer storm. Charging the air with electricity. Bringing with him lightning and thunder
and darkness.

And when he was gone she'd be like those flowers left in the wake of the storm. Flattened. Their
petals torn and ragged.

But standing, she reminded herself. When he left she'd still be standing. As long as she took measures now to toughen herself against the forces of the battering wind and rain.

Chapter 3

Celeste had her morning routine down to a fine art. A steamy shower, followed by a cool spray to wake her. Her hair was cut so perfectly that all it needed was a few flicks of the brush, a quick dry, and every lock fell into place. With her complexion, all that was required was blusher and light eyeliner, followed by lip gloss. She slid her feet into simple bronze pumps and straightened the jacket of her bronze Armani suit, and she was ready for the day.

She picked up her phone to tuck into her pocket and was reminded of the phone message she'd discovered from her grandfather.

"Celeste, darlin'. I've been hearing such good

*things about you and the Old Liberty Tavern. Some
fascinating news. You remember Andrew Hampton? He's with Van Dorn Hotels now. Fine young
fellow. Van Dorn is interested in acquiring a hotel
in New Hampshire. I've given Andrew my blessing
to visit you and observe your operation. Give him
the VIP treatment while he's there. This could be
quite a feather in your cap, darlin' lass. I hear Van
Dorn pays top dollar if they see something they
really want to acquire.''*

Celeste made a mental note to call her grandfather later. He'd sounded oddly elated at the news
that Drew was coming to observe her operation.
And that puzzled her more than she cared to admit.
Why was Grandpa Sully so eager to sell her hotel
to a competitor?

Her hotel.

She stopped in her tracks. She'd taken over the
operation of several failing hotels. Always with the
knowledge that once they were earning their potential, she would move on. So why was this one
different?

In the year she'd been here, she'd taken the Old
Liberty Tavern from the lowest rung of Sullivan
Hotels to a respectable standing, with a better than
average profit statement. But that didn't explain
why it had become this personal crusade. She had
no answer for it. True, she'd poured her heart and
soul into it. But that had been so with every one

of the hotels she'd been sent to restore. Why had this one become different from the rest?

Maybe because of its age and history. It reminded her of so many of the European inns she'd stayed in during her childhood. Maybe it was the town and the people. From the beginning they'd made her feel welcome here. As if she'd come home. As if she were living her childhood dream.

Still, it wasn't like her to want to make one of the Sullivan hotels her own. She'd never before had the inclination to put down roots and stay in one place.

Still shaking her head, she let herself out of her room and locked the door, ready to face another day of nonstop work.

"'Morning. I thought I heard your door opening.''

She turned to find Drew just stepping out of his room. Was it a coincidence? Or had he been waiting for her?

"Good morning." She kept her tone impersonal as she moved toward the elevator.

He pushed the button, then stood back with an admiring glance.

She caught his grin. "What's so funny?"

He shook his head. "Some things never change."

"Such as?"

"The way you always manage to look, even first

thing in the morning, like you're just stepping onto a fashion runway.''

''And you find that funny?''

''I find that amazing.''

She was grateful for the arrival of the elevator. She didn't want to stand here making small talk with him.

As she stepped in and punched the button, she was achingly aware of him standing beside her. Why did he have to look so good? So rugged and earthy, despite the perfectly tailored suit and Italian leather shoes. She would much prefer to concentrate on what had gone wrong between them when they'd parted. But when she looked at him, at that sexy heart-stopping grin, at that teasing glint of humor in his eyes, it wasn't easy to remember the bad times. She found herself forgetting everything except the way she'd felt whenever he kissed her. The way that hard, muscled body felt pressed to hers. The way her heart always seemed to beat faster whenever he touched her.

After that kiss last night, all those old feelings were even closer to the surface. But hopefully, after today, he'd be gone. And she could get back to her life the way it had been before this painful reminder of her past.

As the elevator came to a stop on the main floor

he followed her into the foyer. "Do you have time to share a little breakfast?"

"No." She glanced pointedly at her watch, then headed toward her office. "But thanks anyway."

He watched her walk away, then made his way to the coffee shop. Along the way he stopped in the gift shop. Armed with several newspapers, he settled down to devour the financial sections while enjoying the chef's special breakfast of strawberries dipped in powdered sugar, followed by eggs scrambled with green pepper and onion and a sizzling breakfast steak.

Drew had eaten hotel meals all over the world. He considered himself an expert on what worked in a hotel and what didn't. It occurred to him that the food here at the Old Liberty Tavern was some of the best he'd tasted. Much of it was simple fare. But it was tasty and prepared to perfection.

A little while later he looked up when Jeremiah paused beside his table.

"'Morning, Jeremiah."

"Mr. Hampton. How are your accommodations?"

"First rate, thank you." He indicated the empty chair. "Care to join me?"

"Thank you."

The old man sat down and Drew signaled a waitress who hurried over with a cup of coffee. When she disappeared to fill his order, the old man sat back and sipped gratefully. "I think we have the best coffee in the world right here at the Old Liberty Tavern."

"I think you're right, Jeremiah." Drew looked around. "This is a cozy room. I was just thinking that I like the mix of antiques and collectibles."

The old man nodded. "Miss Celeste's touches can be seen everywhere. Until she came here, this room always seemed cold. She started assembling things from other rooms, that butter churn, the spinning wheel over there, some statuary, rearranging until they looked just right. Then she invited local artists and artisans to display their work along the walls, or on easels. Before you knew it, people were flocking to this room. It became not only a coffee shop, but a place to have a midmorning brunch or a late-night snack. Of course, hiring the best cooks in the business went a long way toward improving it, as well."

The waitress brought his breakfast and he tucked into it while Drew sipped another coffee.

"Our Miss Celeste is amazing."

Drew smiled at the proprietary way the old man spoke of Celeste. As though she had become a treasure to be guarded by the Old Liberty Tavern.

"One day she came across a storeroom and started cleaning it out. When she uncovered an unused fireplace she had it restored. Then she added bookshelves and leather chairs for reading, and next thing we knew she'd turned it into a cozy library for the use of our guests.''

Drew nodded his approval. ''That's clever.''

''Indeed. Now every Sunday evening it's filled for poetry readings. A lot of the local bookstores arrange for their authors to stay overnight at the Old Liberty Tavern while they're on tour. Whenever that happens, we have an overflow crowd.''

Drew smiled. ''Sounds impressive.''

The old man nodded. ''Our Miss Celeste could have hired any number of interior decorators. But she worked with a local decorator to imprint her style on every room and suite in this inn. After she had all the rooms looking the way she wanted, she tackled the courtyard.''

''I've been admiring it,'' Drew admitted.

The old man beamed with pride. ''No one had ever thought to use it for anything except a place to sit in summer. Now she has wine-tastings, concerts, banquets, all under the stars. I tell you, she has the Midas touch. Last month she filled the ballroom for a charity auction that brought celebrities all the way from New York.''

''Careful, Jeremiah.'' Drew's smile widened. ''You're beginning to sound like her public relations firm.''

"You won't find anyone here in Liberty who doesn't sing her praises." He lowered his voice. "A year ago, we all thought we'd seen the end of this old place. It was as close as it's ever come to being boarded up. If that had happened, it would have been sold and these historic old buildings could have been torn down and the land used for an office plaza." He shook his head, clearly distressed at the thought. "It would have been such a crime to destroy a building with such history." He smiled and spread his hands. "Now look at it. It's been given new life."

"I'd say this old building isn't the only thing that's been given a new life."

The old man nodded. "I'll admit it. It would have broken my heart to see the tavern demolished. It's been such a big part of my life. Not to mention the life of our town."

"Then I can see why everyone's so happy. You've saved a piece of history, and brought business back to the town, as well. I'm sure a successful historic old inn means money for the merchants in town."

"It isn't just the money, Mr. Hampton." He studied Drew over the rim of his cup. "Our Miss Celeste restored our sense of pride. A pride that had been missing for a number of years in our town."

When the waitress returned with their bill, Jeremiah reached for his wallet. Drew shook his head. "This is my treat, Jeremiah. I insist."

The old man gave a grudging nod of assent before hurrying away.

When he was alone, Drew thought over all he'd just learned. If it was true that the profits were up, the employees were happy and the town was benefiting from the success of this place, why was Paddy Sullivan considering selling it? Especially in light of Celeste's reaction. It was obvious that she was feeling very territorial about the Old Liberty Tavern.

It was, he realized, just another piece to a very perplexing puzzle.

"What's this?" Celeste looked up from her paperwork when Drew entered her office.

"Coffee and a croissant."

"I don't have time."

"Make time." He set it down in the middle of her papers and poured a healthy amount of cream into her coffee before handing her the cup.

She sipped, then closed her eyes. "Oh, this is wonderful."

"Yeah." He took a seat across from her desk. "Are you aware that your kitchen serves the best coffee around?"

"Of course I am. There isn't anything served in that kitchen that I haven't personally approved." She broke off a piece of croissant and slathered it with strawberry preserves.

"Then I suggest you avail yourself of some of that fine food and beverage from time to time."

She grimaced. "Thank you, Mother."

"You're welcome." He smiled easily. "I had a nice visit with Jeremiah over breakfast this morning. You ought to hire him to handle all your public relations work."

"Isn't he fascinating?" She polished off the last bite of croissant and sipped her coffee. "He's been around this tavern for seventy years or more. And he remembers even the smallest details. I love talking to him."

"So do I. Especially when he talks about 'our Miss Celeste.'"

She laughed. "He is formal, isn't he? It's hard to believe he's known me all my life."

"He has?"

She nodded. "He and my Grandpa Sully used to travel together in their youth. I remember seeing Jeremiah from time to time when he'd be passing through Venice or Paris or Rome. He's been a pilot, a mountain climber, a marathon runner and now I've learned that he even danced on Broadway. But he always returned here to his roots. Our guests really relate to him. He embodies everything good about the Old Liberty Tavern. The sense of history. And that proper New England demeanor. He takes such pride in himself and his work. But he's also comfortable with who and what he is. There are no pretenses about Jeremiah. I see him as the perfect bridge between the old and new. Between what was, and what can be.''

She realized that Drew was watching her closely. Too closely, while she'd allowed herself to ramble.

''Well.'' She set down her empty cup. ''That was just what I needed to restore my energy level. Thanks.'' She pushed away from her desk and crossed to the door. ''Now I'm late for my next appointment. I have to meet with a young couple who want to look over the facilities for their wedding.''

He picked up the tray. ''Don't tell me people still do that.''

''Do what?''

''Get married.''

''Oh.'' She managed a forced smile. ''You'd be surprised. It's becoming quite the trend.''

She breezed out of the office, leaving him alone. Alone.

He'd always hated that word. Maybe because it had defined so much of his life.

He was frowning as he delivered the tray to the kitchen.

A short time later he started down the hall in search of Celeste and her wedding couple. He was, after all, here to observe. It was time he did a little more of that.

"You might want to look through these pictures." Celeste indicated a large, formal album brimming with photographs. "If you're planning a winter wedding, it can be every bit as lovely as a summer event. Not only does the New Hampshire countryside look spectacular under a mantle of snow, with the peaks of the White Mountains in the background, but the Old Liberty Tavern positively glows with warmth inside. We have wood fireplaces blazing with logs in every room. We add pine boughs, and the fragrance makes you think you're in a pine forest. When the millpond freezes we have skaters, and serve hot chocolate around the fire. In the lounge we offer hot mulled wine. And we even have the use of an old-fashioned horse and carriage to transport the wedding party through the town after the ceremony." She flipped through several pictures and pointed to a fur-clad bride and her handsome groom, nestled under a fur throw as they posed in the horse-drawn carriage.

"It makes a lovely centerpiece for a wedding album."

Drew leaned a hip against the table and folded his arms over his chest, watching and listening. The bride- and groom-to-be were clearly enchanted by her sales pitch.

"If you have out-of-town guests coming for the event, we can put them up, so there's no worry about getting lost at the last minute before the ceremony. The ballroom is more than adequate for a grand wedding celebration. And if you prefer something smaller, more intimate, we have a library, or a formal dining room, both of which can be decorated by our expert staff, or by your own party-planner. Also, if you wish to stay on after the others have gone, we have a lovely bridal suite, with a complimentary champagne supper in front of the fire, and a romantic breakfast served in your suite the following morning."

She turned more pages and found a display of elegant wedding cakes. "Our chef can prepare not only the meals, but your cake as well. And our staff can even see to the flowers." She smiled. "We haven't been asked to make a bridal gown yet, or to pick out the rings. But I'm certain we could if asked."

The young couple chuckled, then began leafing through the book.

"Why don't I leave you two alone for a while?" Celeste poured two glasses of complimentary white wine. "Relax. Talk over your plans. Study these price lists. And make note of the things that appeal to you. When I come back, we'll talk some more."

Drew followed her from the room.

When she'd closed the door on the young bride and groom he leaned close to whisper, "Has anyone ever told you that you could sell snow to an Eskimo?"

She arched a brow. "Thank you. I'll take that as a compliment."

"It was meant as one. That was good. As good a pitch as I've ever heard."

"Oh, considering the fact that you're already a vice president of Van Dorn Hotels in just over a year, I'd say you've probably pitched a few good lines of your own."

Instead of feeling insulted, he threw back his head and laughed. "You're right. We're two of a kind, aren't we?"

She flushed slightly. "I used to think so."

"What does that mean?" He paused in the silent, empty hallway.

Instead of pausing beside him she kept on walking toward her office. It took him only two quick strides to catch up with her. He closed a hand over her upper arm, stopping her in her tracks. Though she'd never forgotten the strength in his hands, she was caught by surprise.

"Take your hand off me, Drew."

"Not until you tell me what you meant by that crack."

She lifted a chin in anger. "You didn't used to be so thickheaded."

His eyes narrowed. "And you didn't used to be intentionally cruel. What's this about, Celeste?"

"What is it about?" She slapped his hand aside and stood facing him, fists at her hips. Temper flared in her eyes. "When we met, you convinced me that we were both chasing the same dream. Then I woke up one day and found myself alone."

"I had things I had to do."

"Things that suddenly didn't include me."

"Your name was Sullivan. Mine wasn't."

She drew back as though he'd just slapped her. Her voice chilled by degrees. "I'm sorry that I wasn't enough to make you happy."

"That isn't the issue, and never was. But because your name was Sullivan, I couldn't ask you to leave your family business and go with me. It wouldn't have been fair to ask. Furthermore, if I'd asked, you never would have consented."

She looked down at her hands, then dropped them to her sides. Her tone lost all emotion. "So you just left. And now you're back. Last night you kissed me the way…" She huffed in a breath. "…the way you used to. And I'm supposed to act as though nothing ever happened?"

"What happened…" He was startled by the ringing of his phone. For the space of a moment he actually thought about ignoring it. On the second ring he yanked it out of his pocket. When he saw the identity of the caller he sighed. "It's Eric Van Dorn. I have to take this call."

"Of course you do. We're both very good at keeping our priorities straight, aren't we, Drew?" She took a step back, then turned and headed for her office.

Drew studied the stiff line of her back as he counted to ten and swore softly.

When he had his temper under control he said, "Yes. Drew Hampton here. Good afternoon, Mr. Van Dorn."

As the voice droned on, he headed for the elevator. "I have those figures on my computer. I'll send them along now. And I have a few profit-and-loss comparisons you might want to look at as well."

He punched in the button for the top floor and stared morosely as the numbers flashed past. Once in his room he cradled the phone between shoulder and ear and listened with only half a mind while he scrolled to the file he needed.

"Here it is, sir. I think you'll like the sound of this."

He began reading a list of figures, pausing occasionally while the voice on the other end of the line made a comment.

"I'll send them now. And then I'll get those faxes off to your assistant."

Drew glanced at his watch. If he was lucky, he might get the rest of this paperwork finished by dinnertime. But he'd missed whatever chance he had to set things straight with Celeste.

Maybe that would be the story of their lives. A history of missed opportunities, while they were busy chasing some illusive dream of success.

Chapter 4

Drew stepped out of the elevator to the sounds of a string quartet playing Mozart. The entrance foyer was crowded with people sipping champagne and studying paintings and sculptures that had been artfully arranged along the walls on easels and pedestals.

To handle the flow of guests, additional tables and chairs had been set up in the courtyard, aglow with twinkling lights and hurricane candles.

Drew accepted a glass of champagne from a passing waiter and looked around for Celeste. She was standing with a group of men and women admiring a series of framed oil and acrylic paintings. One of the men was gesturing wildly with his hands. Though Celeste had a smile fixed on her lips, Drew recognized the glazed look in her eyes. She'd probably been on her feet for hours, without a break.

Not his problem, he reminded himself. She was an adult, accustomed to being on her own, and taking care of her own needs. Still, for as long as he'd known her, she'd never been able to put herself first.

Strange, he thought. Anyone looking at her would see a poised, polished, intelligent hotel executive, fluent in several languages, comfortable anywhere in the world. But beneath that polish was a young woman who pushed herself to the limit, often going without sleep, without food, without the basics of life, for the sake of a family business that was already a financial empire.

Why did she feel the need to sacrifice herself? Drew understood what it meant to be driven by ambition. It had been his blessing, or his curse, from the time he was a boy. Having lost his parents at an early age, he'd been consumed with a desperate desire for stability and success. It was that desire that had brought him to the attention of Patrick Sullivan, who had visited the Sullivan Plaza in New York and had taken note of the hardworking college student willing to do any job assigned him. With the elder Sullivan's encouragement, Drew had earned his degree before joining

Sullivan Hotels in Europe. That was where he'd
met Celeste. And had fallen hopelessly in love. He
shook his head, remembering his foolishness. He'd
gone absolutely head-spinning, mind-emptying
crazy over, of all things, the granddaughter of the
president of the company.

What had amazed him, right from the start, even
more than his own foolishness, was her ambition.
An ambition that matched his own.

What drove a young woman who had led such
a charmed life? Swiss boarding schools. Exclusive
summer camps. Trips abroad to study with famous
artists and architects, French chefs, London designers.

She belonged on the boards of Fortune 500 companies. They would be delighted to welcome her.
But here she was, in a little town in New Hampshire, happily working eighteen- and twenty-hour
days in order to make a crumbling, historic inn a
success for the sake of her family empire. Or was
there more to it than that?

Maybe she wasn't doing this simply for the family business. Maybe this filled a need inside herself, as well. A need as deep as his own.

What a pair they were.

"'Evening, Mr. Hampton."

Drew looked up to see Jeremiah Cross beside
him, and wondered how long the old man had been

standing there watching him staring at Celeste like a love-starved teen.

"'Evening, Jeremiah. This is quite a crowd."

The old man nodded. "Getting to be a habit lately." He glanced toward Celeste. "She's been going nonstop since early this morning."

"Yes. So I've noticed."

"The bearded fellow with her is the one who painted those." Jeremiah nodded toward a collection of paintings that appeared to be solid white squares. One had a squiggle of neon yellow directly in the center. The next had a dash of bright pink to one side. A third had black wavy lines running through the white squares. "Calls himself an artist."

Drew grinned. "He's been explaining his art to Celeste since I arrived."

The old man cleared his throat. "You might want to rescue her."

"I might." Drew's smile widened. "Or I might just stand here and see how long she can take the punishment."

The two men shared a quick laugh before Drew snagged a second glass of champagne from a passing waiter. He was doing this to spare the old man, he told himself.

He strolled up to the group clustered around the artist and handed the glass to Celeste. "Here you are, darling."

At the term of endearment, she kept her smile in place while her eyes frosted over. "Drew. Thank you. Have you met Vachel? He was just explaining his art."

"Vachel. Drew Hampton. I've been admiring your work." Drew offered his hand, then turned to Celeste. "I'm afraid you'll have to excuse yourself a moment, darling. There's someone here who's dying to meet you."

She withdrew from the group and followed Drew across the room to a quiet spot.

When they were alone she took a sip of champagne to ease her parched throat. "Thank you."

"Not at all. Jeremiah and I tossed a coin to see who'd play white knight. I lost."

"Yes. That would be a new role for you, wouldn't it?" She handed the glass to him.

"You've lost your taste for champagne?"

"You know I love it. But right now, I have to get out to the courtyard and check on the wait staff."

"Suit yourself." He smiled easily. "But don't blame me if Vachel corners you again and bores you to tears."

"I wasn't bored."

He leaned close. "Tell that to someone who doesn't know you as well as I do, darling."

She kept her smile in place. "Go to hell, darling."

He chuckled as she walked away. Then he drained his glass, all the while watching the sway of her hips. Damned if she didn't have a walk that just made a man itch.

He handed his empty glass to a waiter and slowly circled the room, studying the art that lined the walls, as well as the growing crush of people doing the same thing. It would seem that Celeste was on to something here. There couldn't be this many people in the entire town of Liberty. Which meant that her little soirée had drawn from well beyond the city limits. There was nothing like word of mouth to bring people together. And this particular crowd seemed to be enjoying themselves immensely.

He paused at a seafood buffet table set up in one corner of the room and helped himself to a plate of shrimp, crab and lobster. Happily nibbling, he stepped out into the courtyard and spotted Celeste holding a whispered conference with the head of catering. Minutes later she hurried off. Probably, Drew thought, to handle another crisis.

He glanced up at the star-studded sky. It seemed a shame to waste such a night buried under a mountain of work. But it was her choice. Hadn't work always won out over play?

He thought back to their nights in Rome. Maybe that time had been so special to both of them because it was one of the few times when they'd been able to leave their work, and their responsibilities, behind.

He'd seen a side of Celeste he'd never known. Maybe she'd seen a different part of him, as well. They'd been so happy, so carefree. They'd been like two children set free from school. No restrictions. And wildly in love.

With a frown he handed the plate to a passing waiter and decided to view the rest of the art being exhibited. Maybe it would keep his mind off things better left alone.

She had a right to be angry with him, and skeptical of his return. He'd been the one to walk away. But he'd felt at the time that he had no choice. And now? He wasn't sure what he was doing here now. Was he trying to acquire another hotel for his company? Or was he trying to rekindle an old flame? A flame that he himself had chosen to smother?

Celeste left the now-deserted foyer and stepped into the elevator, pushing the button for the top floor. As soon as the door glided shut she slipped off her shoes and gave a sigh of relief. She was hungry and weary. And she didn't know what hurt more—her feet from standing for so many hours, or her face from smiling at so many strangers.

When the door glided open she picked up her shoes and walked into the hallway, making her way to her door. Just as she was inserting the key she heard a door open behind her and spun around.

"Well, about time." Drew gave her one of his quick, heart-stopping smiles. "I was just about ready to give up on you."

"Give up on..." She shot him a dark look. "Why are you spying on me?"

"Spying? Why, Ms. Sullivan, I'm shocked at your suggestion. Shocked, I tell you." He opened the door wide. "But knowing how you forget to eat, I had room service send up some food."

"I hope you enjoy it." She turned away and fitted her key in her lock.

He stepped closer, his voice taking on a seductive edge. "I have sweet-and-sour chicken. And *Moo Goo Gai Pan.*"

"Moo Goo Gai Pan?" Her eyes widened. "Really?"

"Yeah." He stuck his hands in his pockets and started toward his room. "It's a shame you're not interested."

"Wait." She needed only a second to consider before withdrawing her key and following him.

Inside his room she breathed in deeply. "Oh, it's so unfair. You know exactly how to use my weaknesses against me."

"Yeah." He closed the door and leaned against it, watching as she dropped her shoes and padded toward a table set for two on a small, circular balcony overlooking the courtyard. "Would you care for a little champagne? I snagged a bottle from the art exhibit downstairs."

"I'll remind Bitsy to add it to your bill." She accepted a glass from his hand and sipped. Then she sighed and sipped again. "Oh, it tastes so much better now that the evening is over."

"Evening? This is a whole lot more than evening. Half the night is gone. But who's keeping track?" He walked up to the balcony railing beside her and glanced at the stars. "Can you sleep in tomorrow, or do you have a busload of tourists arriving for a predawn breakfast?"

She laughed. The low, sultry laugh that always seemed to wrap itself around his heart and squeeze until it hurt to breathe. "Am I that bad?"

"Worse. Since I've been here I haven't seen you sit down for more than two minutes without either talking on the phone or handling paperwork."

She nodded. "I know. Sometimes I think I'll take a few hours off. But something always seems to come along."

"Yeah. Like a parade of strangers galloping through the inn like locusts about to devour everything in their path."

"Those locusts pay the bills."

"I bet they do. But they also can drain you of all life's juices if you let them. Speaking of draining…" He motioned toward her empty glass.

She held it out and allowed him to fill it again before glancing skyward. "Mmm. This is nice."

"I'm glad you like it. I ordered it just for you." He indicated a chair. "Why don't you relax and I'll get our food."

"Food. There's that word again." Celeste eased herself into a cushioned rattan chair and watched as Drew carried a covered bowl to the table and began spooning steaming rice and chicken onto their plates.

After the first bite she moaned aloud. "Oh. This is absolutely heavenly. And to think I was going to gulp two aspirin and take myself off to bed."

"Now that would have been a terrible waste. You definitely need some lessons in how to enjoy life, Ms. Sullivan."

She glanced across the table and caught his grin. "And you're volunteering to be my teacher?"

"It's the least I can do." He topped off her champagne and watched with amusement as she spooned more food onto her plate.

"The last I saw of you…" She speared a forkful of chicken. "…you were so busy climbing that corporate ladder, you even considered sleep an intrusion on your valuable time."

"Yeah. Guilty, I admit. But that was before."

"Before what?"

"Before I realized that there are…other things in life." He leaned back, sipping champagne and enjoying the way she looked as she attacked her meal. A gentle breeze caught the ends of her hair before she caught them and tucked them behind her ear. A ribbon of moonlight played over her face and sparkled in her eyes. A faint whiff of her fragrance drifted past, drenching him in memories.

The yearning caught him by surprise.

''What's wrong?'' She looked up and caught an expression on his face that had her fork pausing halfway to her mouth.

''Nothing's wrong.'' He carefully composed his features. ''I just think it would be nice if you'd try to taste some of that before you swallow.''

''No time.'' She cleaned her plate and convinced herself that she'd only imagined that look in his eyes. When she held out her glass for more champagne, he obliged her.

She sipped. ''What's for dessert?''

''Strawberry ice cream.'' He was already on his feet and heading toward the small refrigerator tucked beneath the bar. ''And fortune cookies.''

''Perfect.'' She sighed as he placed a crystal dish in front of her.

She attacked her dessert with the same fervor as the rest of the meal. Then, leaning back, she broke open a fortune cookie and read the tiny slip of paper inside before frowning and tossing it aside without comment.

''Something you ate?''

When she didn't smile he reached across the table and picked up the fortune, reading aloud. "Take time for affairs of the heart." He arched a brow. "Well, now. Excellent advice."

She pouted and drained her glass. "You planted that."

"Of course I did. And then baked the cookie in my spare time."

She burst into laughter. "Okay. Maybe that was stretching it a bit. But you can't deny you're enjoying this."

"So are you. Or were, until you read your fortune."

"You're right. I really was." She drained her glass and got to her feet, giving a last wistful glance at the star-washed sky. "But now it's time to get back to reality."

She stepped from the balcony into his room. There was something so familiar about it. His jacket hung over the back of a chair. His tie tossed carelessly across one end of the sofa. The newspaper sitting on the coffee table. A stack of books next to the lamp beside an overstuffed chair.

She ran a hand over the books, studying the titles. "Who are you reading now?"

He handed her the latest title and she nodded. "I just finished it. I was disappointed with the ending."

He grinned. "Not happy enough for your taste?"

She merely smiled. He knew her so well. They'd always loved the same books. Loved discovering an author who excited them. Loved reading his latest work and then discussing it.

Her smile faded. They'd had so much more in common. Not only in their professional lives, but in their personal lives as well. They shared a love of art, of travel, of exotic food. Maybe that was why the loss seemed so much greater when they'd finally parted.

She picked up her shoes before heading toward the door. With her hand on the knob she turned, only to find him standing directly beside her.

Her heart did a sudden free-fall. "Thanks, Drew. This was a lovely surprise."

"I'm glad you enjoyed it." There it was again. That fleeting scent of wildflowers that always sent his pulse into overdrive.

"I'd better…"

"You could always…"

They both stopped.

She lifted a hand. "You first."

He shook his head. "You were saying?"

"I'd better go." She expelled a breath and turned away, pulling open the door.

Before she could take a step she felt his hand at her shoulder and looked up in surprise. In the space of a heartbeat his hands were grasping her upper arms, dragging her against him as his mouth lowered to hers.

His lips were warm and firm and so very familiar against hers. His mouth moved over hers, sending a rush of heat that slowly dissolved her bones. With the ease of two lovers they came together, taking the kiss deeper. Her shoes slipped from nerveless fingers to land on the floor. Neither of them noticed.

The last time he'd done this, she'd managed to hold herself rigid and deny what she was feeling. This time it was impossible, as a little purr of pleasure hummed in her throat. Her hands seemed to have a will of their own, moving up his chest until they were locked around his neck.

She held on, afraid that if she let go, she would surely drop to the floor in a heap.

"Oh, you feel so good here in my arms. So right." Though this wasn't what he'd planned, there was no denying it was what he'd wanted. Needed. He ran hot nibbling kisses across her cheek to her ear. "Don't go. Stay the night."

Her heart took another sudden dive before fluttering wildly in her chest. "You know I can't."

"You know you want to." His words, whispered in her ear, sent splinters of ice dancing along her spine.

"Oh, Drew. You know me so well." She pulled

back, her hands still linked behind his neck, to look
into those shadowy eyes. "Too well. It would be
so easy to fall back into something that had been
so...easy."

"Not to mention so good between us."

She nodded. "We were good, Drew. But we said
our goodbyes and moved on."

He shook his head. "We didn't move on. We
just moved apart."

"Either way, it would be a mistake to let ourselves slip back now, just for the sake of old
times."

"Is that what you think? That what we felt just
now was...nostalgia? Comfort? Like a pair of old
slippers?"

Before she could respond he dragged her close
and savaged her mouth. With his hands in her hair
he pressed her roughly against the wall and kissed
her again and again until they were both breathless
and trembling.

Now there was no denying what they were both
feeling. Their mouths were greedy, their hands almost bruising as they held on and took each other
on a fast, head-spinning ride. Whatever arguments
they might have had were wiped away in an instant
as they gave themselves up to the pleasure.

When at last Drew lifted his head, his eyes were
dark and fierce, his voice a low rasp of frustration.
"Are you comfortable, Celeste? Are you? Because

I'm sure as hell not. What I'm feeling right now is about as far from comfort or nostalgia as a man can get.''

''What I am is…'' Through sheer effort she kept her voice from trembling. ''…leaving. Right now.''

He stepped back, then bent and retrieved her shoes. Without a word she took them from him and crossed the hall, praying he wouldn't see the way her hand was shaking as she fitted the key in her lock.

She was grateful when the door opened on the first attempt. She stepped inside, then turned to see him standing where she'd left him.

She closed the door and turned the lock. Then she sank down on the floor and leaned her back against the wall, pressing a hand to her eyes. And marveled that she'd found the courage to walk away. When all she'd really wanted was to stay.

Chapter 5

"Grandpa Sully." Celeste's voice warmed as she heard the brogue. "I'm so glad I caught you before going downstairs and getting caught up in the day's work."

"Ah, lass. It's so good to hear from you. I got worried when you didn't return my call."

"To tell you the truth, I forgot to play my messages. I...didn't even know Drew was coming until he was here."

"I see." The voice on the other end of the line paused. "Then you must have been caught by surprise."

"That's putting it mildly." She took a deep

breath. "Grandpa Sully, why would you allow him to observe our operations here?"

"Why not? I didn't think you'd mind, lass. Andrew's an honorable young man. And the firm he's representing is old and reliable."

"But they're our competitors. And he left our company to work for them."

"Spoken like a true Sullivan." He chuckled. "The truth is, Andrew came to me and told me his firm's intentions, and I saw no harm in permitting him a few days to observe."

"He's already had time to observe. I believe he's leaving today." And just in time, she thought. There was no telling what she'd do if she had to be around him any longer.

There was just the slightest pause before Patrick Sullivan said cautiously, "His company's asked for an extension, lass."

"An extension? I don't understand. Why would they ask for more time?"

"Now, now. Not to worry. It's done all the time in business. I hope his being there isn't causing any problems?"

She thought about last night. "No. Of course not."

"Good, lass. That's good. I know it's a bit inconvenient having someone looking over your shoulder. But Andrew will be there and gone before you know it.''

She sighed as the conversation turned to her parents, her sisters, her aunts and uncles. By the time she hung up the receiver, she realized that she'd been given no clear date for Drew's departure.

It didn't matter. She could survive another day or two. Especially since she'd been given no choice in the matter.

"Good morning, Miss Celeste." Jeremiah stood in the foyer wearing a crisp dark suit and sporting a red rose in his lapel. "I'm glad to see you slept in this morning. You've been putting in way too many hours."

She arched a brow. "Are you sure you haven't been talking to Drew, Jeremiah?"

The old man merely smiled. "As a matter of fact, I have been. Mr. Hampton was down early. He and I enjoyed breakfast together. He's a fascinating young man. A clever mind. And a very quick wit."

"Yeah. A laugh a minute." She sighed. "I suppose he's waiting in my office."

"I saw him leaving a while ago. It's such a lovely day, he said he wanted to look around the town."

Celeste breathed a sigh of relief as she walked

away. She'd spent the past hour worrying about how she would react when she saw him again, after that scene last night. Now she'd bought some time.

In her office her assistant looked up. "Good morning, Ms. Sullivan."

"Good morning, Daniel."

He handed her a mountain of mail and phone messages. "The chef asked if you'd stop by the kitchen this morning to discuss some changes in the menu."

"Tell him I'll be there within the hour. What's the status of our linen service?"

"The head of housekeeping reports that since your discussion with Mr. Cormeyer, the deliveries have been on time, and the drivers are being extremely courteous."

"Thank you, Daniel. That's good news." She made her way to her inner office and settled herself behind her desk. As she began the task of returning phone calls and sorting through the mail, she found herself thinking about what Drew had said. It was true that she'd allowed this job to take over her life. But she shouldn't have to apologize for that. After all, she loved her work. Loved working with friendly, fascinating people. Loved the challenge of taking something that was failing, and turning it into a success. She even enjoyed the demanding routine. The mail, the messages, the long lists of things to get done. She was a person who loved making lists, and then checking off items as they were completed. It made her feel productive. She wouldn't know how to live without the demands of a satisfying career.

Still, how long had it been since she'd taken a day off to do nothing more than browse through an antique shop, or sit at a sidewalk café in town and linger over a sinfully rich dessert?

She gave a huff of breath. What foolishness. There was a time to work and a time to play. Right now, she had to remain focused on the job at hand. She finished her paperwork, glanced at her watch and shoved away from her desk.

In the outer office she called, "Daniel, if you need me, I'll be in the kitchen conferring with Marcus."

She decided to take a shortcut through the courtyard. It was such a pretty day. Not a cloud in the sky to mar the sunshine. Just the slightest breeze, carrying the perfume of flowers. One of the staff was watering all the carefully tended flower beds. They glistened like pretty jewels in the sunlight.

In the kitchens she watched as the head chef studied a faxed list of prices from a food whole-saler and checked off the items he wanted to order.

He looked up when she approached. "Good morning, Ms. Sullivan."

"Good morning, Marcus. You wanted to talk to me about some changes in the menu?"

He nodded and set aside his paperwork. "The summer produce is reaching its peak. This morning at the farmer's market I was able to get a good price on tomatoes and garden greens, so I'll be offering some special salads for the next few weeks."

"That's fine." Celeste knew the value of a good chef, and Marcus was one of the best. He took his job as seriously as she did. In fact, several mornings each week he stopped at the local farmer's market before planning the chef's specials for the week. "But you know you don't need my permission to plan your menu."

"I know that. But I wanted to ask you how you enjoyed your meal last night, since it was something I've never offered on the menu. Drew Hampton told me the sweet-and-sour chicken and *Moo Goo Gai Pan* are favorites of yours. I'd like to know how they measured up."

She flushed, realizing she'd barely taken the time to taste anything before wolfing it down. Still, it had been marvelous. "Marcus, I assure you they were as good as any I've eaten anywhere in the world."

The chef beamed. "Then with your permission, I'd like to consider adding them to the menu from time to time."

She nodded. "Why don't you give it a try and see how those selections go over with our guests?"

"Thanks. I will." The man was positively beaming. After all, food was his life. He took such pride in his work. And treasured every compliment. "By the way, if you get into Liberty later, you might want to check out the farmer's market yourself. They have some flowers that would be dazzling in the courtyard."

"Flowers?"

"Giant pots of begonias that would look great in that area shaded by the umbrella tables."

She wasn't surprised that an artist like Marcus would have an eye for such beauty. But she was pleased that his sense of pride extended to other areas besides the kitchen. "Thanks. Maybe I'll take the time to check them out."

As she walked away it occurred to her that, though she hadn't planned on giving up an hour of her precious time, it wouldn't be wasted. She would visit the farmer's market, pick up the flowers and be back before lunch.

Drew wandered the town, determined to stay away from the Old Liberty Tavern for the entire day. He needed some space. Needed to put some distance between himself and Celeste.

What was he going to do about her? Had he really thought that seeing her again would somehow end this ache in his heart? Maybe he'd foolishly believed that things would be different between them now that they'd had some time apart. He'd hoped that he would be able to look at her and see nothing more than a sharp, savvy businesswoman who had no time for anything except the pursuit of the next prize. But nothing had changed. Whenever he looked at her, he wanted her. Maybe it was because they were so alike. Or maybe he was still that little boy, wanting what he couldn't have. But he suspected it went much deeper. Time and distance hadn't put an end to the yearning. From the time they'd first met, he'd sensed that they were a perfect fit. Seeing her again made her even more aware of it.

He paused outside a gift shop and studied the display of antique cars alongside a poster of the Grand Prix. He found himself wishing Celeste could see it. It would be the perfect addition to the coffee shop, behind the cash register.

As he moved along the sidewalk he realized that behind this sleepy small-town facade was a lively, bustling town just filled with fascinating shops, cozy restaurants, interesting galleries. As he am-bled farther along the street, he decided that before he left, he would acquaint himself with every one of them. It would, after all, add another dimension to his report.

"Here you go, miss." A deeply-tanned farmer in plaid shirt and overalls handed Celeste a basket as she made her way through the stalls of colorful flowers and foliage. She looped the handle of the basket over her arm and breathed deeply, feeling like a child in a toy shop. The air was perfumed with the fragrance of hundreds of blossoms. If she could, she would buy all of them and surround herself with their beauty. She had an absolute weakness for flowers.

"I'm looking for the begonias."

"Over here, miss." The farmer's wife led her along row after row of flowers in every imaginable hue. Petunias ranging in color from deepest purple to palest pink. Dark burgundy spikes and dull-gold primroses. Bloodred climbing roses. Delicate white baby's breath.

"Here you are, miss. There's a lot to choose from."

Celeste caught her breath at the jewel tones of the rose-shaped blossoms and glossy foliage massed in huge pottery urns. They'd been cleverly planted to show off the blooms in the best possible light, with a nice mix of color and texture, taller flowers and low hanging vines trailing to the ground. Marcus was right. These would be the perfect addition to the courtyard.

"Do you think you could deliver these to the Old Liberty Tavern?"

The old woman smiled. "That's not a problem. How many would you like?"

Celeste mentally calculated, seeing them massed here and there for the best possible effect. "A dozen, I believe." She withdrew a card from her purse.

The woman took her card and hurried away, returning minutes later with a receipt. "We can have them there within the hour, miss."

"Thank you." Celeste glanced at the empty basket on her arm. "Now maybe I'll just walk through the cut flowers and see if anything catches my eye."

She started toward a stall displaying hundreds of bouquets, picturing in her mind a bouquet in the foyer, another in the lobby, and a third in her office. Within minutes the basket was brimming with multi-colored Shasta daisies, white and yellow roses, and delicate baby's breath. She was reaching over to help herself to half a dozen vines of trailing ivy when she heard a voice.

"Well, if you aren't a sight."

She looked up to find Drew walking toward her. In his hand was a bouquet of long-stemmed red roses.

"Drew." She could feel warmth rushing to her cheeks. "I didn't expect to see you at a farmer's market."

"I might say the same for you." He glanced at the basket brimming with blossoms. "I know you're dedicated to your job, but don't tell me you actually choose all the flowers for your hotel each day."

She laughed and shook her head. "I guess it looks that way. Actually I came here because Marcus, our chef, told me about some great planters. After ordering them for the courtyard, I just got carried away and decided to buy fresh flowers while I was here." She stared pointedly at the roses in his hand. "It looks like you did, too."

"Yeah." He glanced down, then thrust them toward her. "I bought them for you. I know how much you love roses."

"Oh, Drew." She gathered them close and breathed in their fragrance. "They're beautiful."

"They don't hold a candle to the woman who's holding them."

She was grateful for the arrival of the farmer's wife at that moment. The presence of a stranger saved her from blubbering, or possibly throwing her arms around his neck and making a complete fool of herself.

The old woman eyed the mass of flowers. "Would you like me to have these sent to the tavern along with the rest of your delivery?"

Celeste had to resist the foolish desire to cling to the roses. How long had it been since a man had given her flowers? Too long. Probably not since Rome, when Drew had paused at a flower vendor and had filled her arms with roses. They'd walked through the rain-washed streets, laughing like fools, so wildly in love they didn't care if the whole world knew it.

She looked up to find both Drew and the old woman staring at her.

"Yes." She was aware of a catch in her voice, and hoped they didn't notice. "That would be nice." She handed over the roses, then slid the basket from her arm. "And these, as well."

When the woman was gone she was aware that Drew was still watching her a little too carefully. To cover her embarrassment she gave a short laugh. "It looks like we both got carried away by the smell of all these flowers. But they won't go to waste back at the tavern."

"Don't you know that beautiful things are never a waste? Or have you never heard the expression beauty is its own excuse for being?" He started along the path toward the entrance to the farmer's market and turned to see her standing still, watching him.

He gave her a smile and waited until she caught up to him. "Did you drive here?"

"No. I walked."

"So did I." He turned. "Do you have to get back? Or can you spare some time?" He took advantage of her hesitation. "I passed a really interesting looking café with an outdoor patio. I'll bet you didn't take time for breakfast this morning. How about a quick lunch before you head back?"

It was on the tip of her tongue to refuse. But he had already tucked his arm through hers and was leading her along the sidewalk. What was the harm? she argued. It was a slow day at the tavern, with nothing requiring her absolute attention. Besides, the sun was shining. The air was perfumed with flowers. And her heart was feeling lighter than it had in ages.

"I think I could manage a half hour."

Celeste polished off the last of her fresh seafood salad and sipped her second cup of tea. She and Drew had lingered for more than two hours at the pretty little outdoor café, watching the passing parade of people hurrying by with shopping bags and attaché cases.

"I like this town." Drew sat back and stretched out his long legs, feeling more relaxed than he had in months. "There's just a nice solid feel to it. Have you noticed?"

Celeste nodded. "I felt it the moment I got here. It's strange." She looked around at the clean street, the interesting array of buildings, some ancient, some modern, but all pleasing to the eye. "When I first got here, I felt as if I'd been here before."

"I know what you mean. In some ways it's probably like every other small town in the world. But there's something unique here."

"That's it exactly." It pleased her to know that he shared her feelings about the town. "I can't put my finger on it yet, but I feel good just walking down the street. Which reminds me..." She glanced at her watch. "I'd better get back to work."

"Before you go, there's something I'd like to show you." Drew paid their bill and took her arm.

They made their way along the main street, peeking into windows, pausing to admire displays.

"Oh." Celeste suddenly caught his hand and led him across the street to a bakery. "Smell that."

They stood outside the little shop and breathed in.

"Cinnamon." Drew grinned. "You could never resist cinnamon."

"And raisins. Look." She pointed to a woman placing a tray of freshly baked cookies in the display window.

Celeste started inside, with Drew following. Minutes later they emerged with a sack of cookies.

Drew was laughing as she dug her hand into the bag and removed an oversized cinnamon-raisin oatmeal cookie.

She bit into it and closed her eyes. "Umm. Here." She held it to his mouth until he took a bite.

"You realize, don't you, that they saw you coming?" He was grinning at her. "They set that tray in the window to lure you in."

"I know." She took another bite and continued nibbling as she walked along beside him. "They probably even opened a window somewhere and fanned the air so I'd smell that cinnamon. But I don't mind at all." She sighed and reached into the bag for another. "Do you know how long it's been since I tasted freshly baked cinnamon-raisin cookies?" She thought a minute then added, "I think probably eight or nine years ago, when my Grandma Sullivan baked them."

"Didn't you get the recipe?"

She laughed. "A lot of good that would do me. You know I never bother to cook or bake for myself."

"Yeah. As I recall, you leave that up to your sister, Lizbeth."

"Our little homemaker." Celeste stopped and shot him a smile. "You've just given me a great idea. I know what I'll ask her to send me for my birthday."

They paused outside the shop he'd seen earlier. He pointed to the window display. "Isn't that great? I love the contrast between the antique cars and the poster of last year's Grand Prix."

She nodded enthusiastically. "So do I. And I have the perfect spot to showcase it."

"In the coffee shop behind the cash register."

She turned to him with a look of astonishment. "How did you know I'd say that?"

He touched a finger to the tip of her nose. "Because we think alike." He bent and brushed a featherlight kiss across her cheek. "And because it's exactly what I thought when I first saw it. And I was fairly certain you'd agree."

She absorbed the little jolt before turning away and starting into the shop, with Drew trailing behind.

Minutes later they emerged carrying the poster rolled into a cardboard tube tucked under Celeste's arm, and the antique cars in a shopping bag which Drew carried.

"Happy?" he asked.

"Very."

It was true, she realized. With nothing more than a simple lunch, a bag of cookies and a few trinkets, she was feeling more relaxed than she had in years.

How long had it been since she'd walked through a town and lingered in a shop or picked up something at the bakery? Too long, she realized. But, if she were going to be honest with herself, it was more than the sunny day or the pretty town. The reason for her joy was the man beside her. With Drew, everything seemed more. More relaxing. More pleasure at his simple teasing. More laughter.

"Ready to start back to the tavern?"

His words brought her out of her reverie. "Not really. How about you?"

Now where had that come from? It was completely out of character for her to say or do anything spontaneous. But just being here with Drew, feeling so gloriously free, had done something to her brain. She suddenly wanted, more than anything in the world, to prolong the pleasure for a little while longer.

Drew stopped to look at her before giving a casual shrug of his shoulders. "My time is your time, Ms. Sullivan. What did you have in mind?"

She couldn't hold back the laughter that erupted. "Oh, Drew, that's such a leading question, I'm tempted to say something that would have us both blushing. However..." She swallowed back the smile that played at the corner of her lips. "...what I have in mind is exploring a few more shops, and maybe enjoying dinner here in town."

If he was surprised, he kept his feelings to himself. "What about your work?"

She touched a hand to her purse. "My phone hasn't rung once, which tells me that so far we've dodged any crises. Who knows? Maybe we can even get through the afternoon without a single interruption."

"Okay, Ms. Sullivan." He smiled and caught her hand in his before pointing to a row of shops across the street. "Time's a-wasting. Let's get started."

Chapter 6

The sun hovered just behind the church spire, shooting brilliant red and bronze sparks across the roofs of the houses below. For a few brief moments the streets appeared to be paved with gold. Then the sun dipped lower, casting the town of Liberty in pale lavender shadows.

Celeste and Drew sat watching the spectacular sunset from their position in the cozy alcove of a little Italian restaurant. On a shelf nearby stood an array of shopping bags and parcels, giving testimony to a day spent browsing every store and gallery in the town.

A waiter poured two glasses of red wine, then discreetly disappeared, leaving them sitting side by side.

Drew gave her an admiring look. "You really know how to shop, lady."

She smiled. "You're not half bad yourself. I love the little copper frog. What are you going to do with him?"

"I have the perfect spot for him." He paused. Sipped. "I thought you could put him on that little pedestal shelf you picked up in the gallery."

She arched a brow. "I was going to hang that shelf in my office, behind my desk."

"Yeah. That's what I figured." He grinned. "With my silly little frog sitting on it, you'll have a reason to smile every morning before you tackle all that paperwork."

"You bought him for me?" She felt an unexpected warm glow at the knowledge.

"Just returning the favor. I still have that frog tie you bought me. Remember?"

She shot him a look of surprise. "You do?"

"You told me your life would be easier if I were as homely as a frog. And I said I'd work on it." His smile became a rumble of laughter. "I still wear it whenever I need cheering up."

"Not to board meetings, I hope."

"And why not?"

"Somehow I can't picture the chairman of the board of Van Dorn Hotels ever considering elevating to the role of president a man who wears a goofy frog tie to board meetings."

"Ha. That's how much you know about it. The chairman of Van Dorn Hotels happens to like my frog tie. He said it shows me to be a man of sensitivity and good taste." Drew took another sip of wine before adding, "I believe he said that just before he stuck out his tongue and caught two flies."

Celeste was still laughing when the waiter came to take their order. It occurred to her that she hadn't laughed this much in ages. But then, she and Drew had always brought out each other's silly natures.

A short time later, as evening shadows thickened and darkness began to cover the land, she and Drew shared a wonderful antipasto and salad before sipping more wine. Then they feasted on veal and pasta kissed with just a hint of garlic.

When their table was cleared the waiter asked, "Would the lady and gentleman care for dessert or espresso?"

Drew finished the last of his wine. "The lady can always make room for dessert. And we'll both have espresso."

The waiter returned with a plate of tiramisu, a pastry filled with rich cream and lined with lady fingers, and two steaming cups of espresso, before leaving them alone.

"Oh, Drew. You have to taste this." After one bite, Celeste lifted the fork to his mouth and watched his reaction.

He nodded. "It's positively sinful." He shook his head in disbelief. "Where do you put all this food?"

"I really don't know. In fact, since you've been here, I've eaten more than I normally would in a month." She took another bite. "I can see that you're a very bad influence on me."

"Uh-huh." He watched as she finished the dessert, and drained her cup of espresso. "Are you sure you aren't hiding a storage tank under that jacket?"

"Oh, no." She patted her middle. "Now you've discovered my secret. Swear you won't tell a soul?"

"Hmm." His smile widened. "I'll think about it. In the meantime, I think we'd better walk off some of this food."

"Great idea." She stood and began to gather up their packages while he settled the bill.

Once outside they turned away from the town and started toward the Old Liberty Tavern, whose weathered roofline glinted in the moonlight.

Celeste looped her arm through Drew's. "That dessert was fabulous. I'm going to have to talk to Marcus about getting the recipe. If we offered it at the tavern, I doubt we could keep up with the demand."

He closed a hand over hers. "Do you know that's the first time you've mentioned work in hours?"

"Is it?" She fell silent, digesting that fact.

It had indeed been hours since she'd given a thought to the business. She'd phoned her assistant only once, to tell him that she wouldn't be returning to the office. If Daniel had sounded a little surprised, he'd managed to cover it quickly. After that, she'd put him and the work awaiting her, out of her mind.

It had felt good to get away. To forget, for almost an entire day, the weight of responsibility that was so much a part of her life. The decisions, the paperwork, the endless meetings, would still be there in the morning, tugging at her mind. But for now, she felt a lightness she hadn't known in a very long time.

"Smell that air." She lifted her face and breathed deeply.

"Yeah." He linked his fingers with hers. "I was thinking how clean and fresh it is here. No auto exhaust fumes stinging the eyes."

"And have you noticed how quiet it is?"

He nodded. "No planes, trains or automobiles. I feel like I'm on vacation in the Alps."

She grinned. "Only better. You can speak the language here."

"You," he said, squeezing her hand, "can speak the language just about anywhere."

"Well, not in China."

"Yet."

They both laughed.

When they reached the front steps of the tavern, Celeste climbed the first step, so that she was almost eye level with him. "I had a wonderful time today, Drew. Thanks to you."

"I'm glad my last day here was so pleasant."

"Your...last day?" She absorbed the blow to her heart. She'd almost forgotten the fact that he was only here for a short time. "You're leaving in the morning?"

He nodded. "My company offered me more time, but I think I've seen enough to make a report. If I need any more documentation, you can fax it."

He was grateful for the shopping bags and parcels. This time, he intended to keep his hands to himself, instead of having them on her. That always got him into trouble, he realized. Last night, the minute he'd touched her, he'd been lost. And then he'd made a fool of himself, asking her to stay the night. As he'd replayed it in his mind later, it had sounded a lot like begging. Not a pleasant thing to admit. Especially to a proud man.

Not this time. Since this was his last night in town, he was determined to keep things light. Light and friendly.

He gave her a smile. "If you want, I can drop these things at your office."

She shook her head and took a step closer. "I'll

summon one of the bellmen. They can use a pass-
key to leave them in my suite upstairs.''

''It's no trouble to take them, Celeste....'' The
words died in his throat as she let the packages
slide to the porch before wrapping her arms around
his neck and brushing her lips over his.

For the space of several seconds he stood perfectly still, his fingers frozen to the packages in his
hands. But when she pressed her body to his and
took the kiss deeper, he released his hold on the
bags and parcels, allowing them to fall to his feet.
Then his arms came around her and he lifted her
off the ground and kissed her until her head was
spinning.

Had the earth tilted? She didn't know. All she
knew was that there was an explosion of fireworks
going off behind her closed eyes. And the hunger
she felt for him was suddenly so compelling, she
wanted to devour him here on the spot.

''Oh, Drew.'' The two words came out in a long,
drawn out sigh. ''I didn't realize you were leaving
in the morning. What am I going to do about you?
What are we going to do about...this?''

''This?''

''This...sizzle between us.''

''Oh yeah. This...sizzle. What would you like
to do?'' He kept his mouth on hers, lowering her
gently until her feet touched the ground.

She shook her head and nuzzled his jaw until he thought he'd go mad from wanting her lips. Finally she turned her head enough to capture his mouth with hers.

Against his lips she whispered, "What I'd like to do isn't the same as what's sensible."

"Forget sensible. What would you like to do?"

"I'd like you to take me up to your room and make mad, passionate love until morning."

She'd just described heaven. He could feel his heartbeat racing like a runaway train.

Still he managed to lift his wrist until he could see his watch and attempt a lightness he didn't feel. "Okay. If you insist, I'll just have to sacrifice my body for your happiness. But I really wanted to watch a midnight marathon of cartoons."

She laughed and pressed her cheek to his. "Oh, I've missed your silliness. Why do you have to be so damnably agreeable?"

"Anyone homely as a frog has to have some redeeming virtue." He caught her lower lip between his teeth. "Mine is that I'm too damned easy for my own good."

Out of the corner of his eye he saw Bitsy Hillerman stepping out the front door of the tavern.

Against Celeste's temple he whispered, "Don't look now but there's a spy in our midst. Come on. Let's sneak away while there's still time."

"Wait. I..." Celeste looked up to see the young woman gaping at them.

"Good evening, Ms. Sullivan." Bitsy's voice was a squeak of embarrassment.

"'Evening, Bitsy." Celeste took a step away and bent to retrieve her parcels.

Suddenly Jeremiah appeared on the porch. Almost, Drew thought, as though he'd been watching, and was annoyed at Bitsy's interruption.

The old man sent Bitsy on her way, then turned to Celeste and Drew. "If you'd like, I'll take these packages to your room, and the two of you can go about your business."

"Our business?" Celeste felt as if she'd just been doused with a bucket of ice water. Her sensible nature returned. And with it, the realization of what she'd almost done. In the afterglow of a lovely day she'd almost made an irrational decision that later would have caused both of them extreme discomfort.

She brought her mouth to Drew's ear and whispered firmly, "Looks like you've just been saved by the cavalry." She took a step back, keeping her gaze steady on Drew's as she called, "Thank you, Jeremiah. I'd appreciate that. If anyone asks, I'll be in my office. Good night, Jeremiah. Good night, Drew."

She never looked back as she started up the steps.

The old man looked from one to the other in consternation, then retrieved the packages and followed her.

When he was alone, Drew felt a wave of frustration and decided what he needed was a long walk in the courtyard. He shoved his hands in his pockets and turned away, breathing deeply of the cool night air. And praying it would help clear his mind.

What had just happened here? Was it just incredibly bad timing? Or was there some cosmic force working against them? Whatever the case, being this close to Celeste, and not being able to have her, was driving him around the bend. It was a good thing this was his last night here. Neither of them would be safe, it seemed, until they had a few thousand miles between them.

The ringing of Drew's phone had him struggling through a layer of deep sleep.

"Hmmm?" He held the receiver to his ear, keeping his eyes shut.

"Andrew?" The booming brogue of Patrick Sullivan had him sitting straight up in bed.

"Yes."

"Did I wake you, lad?"

"Uh." He dragged a hand through his hair and managed a smile. "Yes."

"Sorry. I was talking with Eric Van Dorn, and

he suggested I speak with you directly. Are you ready to make a recommendation to your board?''

"I...suppose I am.''

"Before you do, I'd like to meet with you.''

"Meet with me? In Venice?''

"No. No. I'll be flying up to New Hampshire. Would you mind staying until I get there?''

Drew almost groaned. He felt like he was riding a roller coaster that never ended. Every day he spent with Celeste was another test of his willpower. And now he was being asked by Patrick Sullivan himself to remain in temptation's path.

"I guess I could arrange to stay another day or so.''

"Good, lad. Good. I'll see you...probably before the weekend.''

The line went dead, and Drew stared at the bedside clock, knowing it would be impossible to fall back to sleep now. The thought of the woman sleeping just across the hall had him climbing out of bed and heading to the shower. As if, he thought, wryly, even cold water would do any good at all.

The Old Liberty Tavern was hosting back-to-back conferences. The first was an artists' conference, filling every guest room, conference room, and banquet facility, and putting considerable strain on the overworked staff. The attendees held seminars, workshops and an award banquet that filled the ballroom. The conference culminated in a much-publicized showing of art that brought fans from around the country to bid on favorite pieces.

No sooner had that demanding group checked out than a conference of professional business-women checked in, and once again the staff was forced to step up its pace.

As Drew settled himself at a small table in the rear of the crowded coffee shop, it occurred to him that he hadn't seen Celeste except in passing for more than three days. And he hadn't heard another word from Patrick Sullivan.

"Good morning, Mr. Hampton."

Drew looked up to find Jeremiah, looking dapper in a black, double-breasted jacket with a white handkerchief in his breast pocket, and a white carnation in his lapel.

"'Morning, Jeremiah. Do you have time to join me?"

"I believe I do." The old man pulled out a chair and signaled a waitress for a cup of coffee.

Minutes later she set a steaming cup in front of him and took his order.

He looked around the room. "Busy time of year. I don't believe I've ever seen so many attractive women in one place."

Drew smiled. "I hadn't noticed."

Jeremiah studied him. "Usually when a man

doesn't notice a room full of beautiful women it's because one woman already owns his heart.''

When Drew made no response the old man lifted his cup and drank before setting it down carefully. ''Did you hear that our Miss Celeste has been asked to participate in a workshop for the current organization in residence?''

''No, I hadn't heard.'' Drew sipped his own coffee. ''But I'm not surprised. If anyone knows about being a professional, it's Celeste. I'm sure she'll have some good advice she's willing to share.''

''Would you like to attend her workshop?''

Drew shook his head as a waitress served their breakfast. ''I doubt I'd be welcome at a professional women's conference.''

''Oh, I don't know about that. As a guest of the Old Liberty Tavern, you're welcome to go anywhere on the premises without asking for any sort of special treatment.'' Jeremiah tasted his vegetable omelette and helped himself to wheat toast. ''How much longer do you think you'll be here, Mr. Hampton?''

Drew shrugged. ''I should have been gone days ago. But a phone call changed my plans.''

Jeremiah studied him from beneath those trim white brows, then drained his coffee and smiled before getting to his feet. ''It's time for me to get back to work. As usual, I've enjoyed your company, Mr. Hampton.'' He started away, then turned back. "In case you're interested, Miss Celeste's workshop is a panel discussion with several other high-powered executives. I believe the subject is 'What Price Success?'." He cleared his throat. "It's being held in the Franklin Pierce Room in half an hour."

Drew watched as the old man threaded his way through the bustling crowd. Then he glanced at his watch. It wouldn't hurt to just drop by for a few minutes and hear Celeste's views on the price she considered necessary for success.

Celeste checked her makeup and hair, then picked up her notes and made her way to the conference room. She wasn't particularly nervous about being part of a panel discussion. Public speaking never rattled her. And in this instance, she was pleased to have been invited to share her views with other businesswomen.

When she reached the Franklin Pierce Room she made her way slowly toward the front, pausing to meet and greet dozens of women along the way. By the time she'd made it to the long table lined with microphones, several other panelists were already seated.

While the moderator introduced the panel and listed their many achievements, Celeste took a moment to scan the crowd. So many women. And all of them had worked their way to positions of importance in the companies of their choice. It felt good to be counted among their number.

Soon she was deeply involved in a lively panel discussion, fueled by written questions submitted by the attendees, on matters ranging from the importance of post-graduate degrees to how to demand a salary commensurate with ability. Before long the discussion moved from the dangers of professional friendships to the price many women paid in their personal lives while striving to reach the top of the corporate ladder.

A young, beautiful executive in charge of special affairs for an international banking conglomerate remarked that she was never in one place long enough to develop a relationship. She ended by saying that the great love of her life had grown weary of waiting for her, and had married someone else.

"Ms. Sullivan?" The moderator turned to her. "Do you have any advice?"

Celeste adjusted her microphone. "I think you're tormenting yourself needlessly. If he really loved you, he'd have understood your need to pursue your goals even if he didn't share them, and he would have been willing to wait as long as it took."

"Even if it took forever?" a member of the audience called.

There was a smattering of laughter, and Celeste

smiled before adding, "Yes. Even if it took forever. If two people really love each other, they'll find a way to work things out. No matter how complicated."

The moderator glanced at her watch and stepped to the microphone. "I guess Ms. Sullivan's opinion will be the last word on the subject. I'm afraid we're out of time. I'll remind you that due to the beautiful weather, lunch today will be in the courtyard."

Celeste gathered up her notes and got to her feet. As she did, she spotted Drew seated in the very last row. At that moment he stood and began making his way with the rest of the crowd toward the door.

She started after him, threading her way through the crowd. She was forced to pause with every step to accept congratulations or to speak to clusters of women she knew. By the time she made it to the door, Drew was nowhere to be seen.

She heard a woman's voice beside her saying to a friend, "If I had something like that waiting for me, I might be persuaded to give up my career, my paycheck and even my future with the company."

Her friend made a purring sound of agreement.

Celeste turned to see what they were looking at. Drew was standing in a circle of women. Whatever he'd said had drawn nods of agreement, along with the warmth of bubbling laughter.

She felt a rush of feeling that startled her. Jealousy? It couldn't be. She didn't have a jealous bone in her body.

Still...

As she watched the way the women interacted with him, she felt a bristle of resentment. They were practically drooling.

She turned away and headed toward her office. She'd wasted enough time. Let those silly women make fools of themselves if they wanted. As for her, she had calls to return, and paperwork to deal with.

Oh why, she thought with a fresh wave of annoyance, hadn't Drew left on schedule?

And if he had to stay longer, why couldn't he look like a frog?

Chapter 7

"Bitsy." Celeste paused by the front desk. "You're putting in a late night, too, I see."

"I don't mind." The college student stifled a yawn. "Our night clerk had a big date tonight, and I told him I'd cover for him. There's not that much to do. Most of the conference attendees have turned in for the night. There are a few still gathered in the pub." She gestured toward the sound of voices coming from the adjoining room. "How about you, Ms. Sullivan? Ready to call it a night?"

"Not quite yet." Celeste smiled. "But soon, I hope."

She headed toward the courtyard and paused beside the new urns, admiring the way they looked in the moonlight. Marcus had been right. They were a perfect addition to the other plantings, adding just the right touch of color and texture.

Smiling her approval she turned and let out a quick breath at the sight of Drew directly behind her, nearly hidden in the shadows.

"You startled me. I didn't see you there."

He got to his feet. "I was just enjoying a cigar and brandy. Care to join me?"

"Well, I might like some brandy, but I'll pass on the cigar."

He chuckled as he held her chair. "All right. I'll see what I can do. Would you like me to light the candle?"

She shook her head as she settled herself. "If you don't mind, I prefer the darkness."

"Good. So do I."

She watched as he went in search of a waiter. Smoke drifted from the ashtray on the table, where he'd left his cigar. She found it oddly comforting. Maybe, she thought, because her father and grandfather had always enjoyed a cigar late at night, after a long day of work.

Within minutes Drew returned with a second snifter of brandy. He handed it to her before taking the seat beside her.

"Here's to warm summer nights." He touched his glass to hers.

She felt the pleasant rush of heat and wondered

why she'd never been able to feel this way with any other man.

"I thought you'd be enjoying the company of all those women in the pub. You're missing a wonderful opportunity to be the center of attention."

He shook his head. "Too much estrogen for my taste. I'd be badly outnumbered in there."

"So you're hiding out here."

"Just enjoying the stars." He glanced heavenward. "You ought to try it now and then. It's good for the soul."

She followed suit and tipped back her head. "Okay. I'm looking. I hope this satisfies…" The clever words she was about to say slipped away into silence.

He turned his head and caught the expression of awe on her face. "Stunning, isn't it?"

"It really is. I hadn't realized just how beautiful the night sky can be here in our little courtyard."

"I don't think I've seen a prettier sight anywhere in the world."

At the unusual gruffness in his tone she turned to see him staring, not at the sky, but at her. Not even the darkness could hide the look in his eyes.

Her own voice lowered to a whisper. "Don't, Drew."

"Don't what? Say what I mean?" He touched a hand to her arm. Just the lightest of touches, but she could feel the heat race through her veins.

"Why shouldn't I? You have to know how I feel, Celeste. I've made no secret of it."

"I know that we have a shared history...."

"Is that all we have? A shared history?"

"You know what I mean." She took a sip of brandy to soothe her suddenly dry throat. "I suppose it's always awkward when two old..." She hated to say the word. It sounded so trite. But she knew of no other way to say it. "...when two old lovers are forced to confront each other again. But that doesn't mean we can't be friends."

"Is that what you want? That we be friends?"

"I..." She set down her glass because her hand was shaking slightly. "Yes."

"All right." He offered his hand. "Friends."

She shot him a quizzical look as she placed her hand in his. But when he surprised her by lifting it to his lips, she couldn't hide the little shiver that danced along her spine. She withdrew her hand and clenched it firmly in her lap.

"You know just what buttons to push, don't you, Drew?"

"I could say the same about you."

She shook her head. "I'm not the one who's trying to seduce you before you leave."

"Aren't you?" He got to his feet and jammed his hands in his pockets to keep from touching her again. "What would you call that little scene on the front steps a few nights ago?"

She shoved back her chair and stood facing him. "We'd just spent a wonderful day together. I wanted to thank you."

"That was some thank you." His voice lowered to a whisper. "I believe you invited me to carry you up to my room and make mad, passionate love all night. Tell me. Does the offer still stand?"

Having her own words flung back at her had her stinging with embarrassment. She was still humiliated, and more than a little puzzled, by her behavior that night.

She turned away. "I don't know what got into me. I don't usually act like such a fool."

"A fool? Is that how you see yourself?" He turned her roughly to face him. His eyes, which minutes ago had been cool and controlled, were now narrowed in anger. "I used to know how to read you, Lessie."

His use of that old nickname was an arrow straight to her heart.

"But not anymore. Now you blow hot one minute, cold the next. If I didn't know you better I'd think I was dealing with some repressed virtuous maiden of old who wanted to experience the joy of sex without the sting of guilt." He closed his fingers around her chin and forced her to look at him. "Is that what this is about? Protecting your virtue?"

"Damn it, Drew. It isn't my virtue I'm trying to

protect.'' She felt the hot sting of tears, which only added to her humiliation. ''It's my heart.''

There was a stunned silence.

The minute the words were out of her mouth she regretted them. But it was too late to call them back. Now she'd simply have to tough it out.

''Your...?'' He stared down at her with a look of astonishment.

She lifted her chin. ''When you left me, I thought my heart would never heal.'' She bit her lip to keep it from trembling. ''And I vowed I'd never let you or anyone else do that to me again.''

He framed her face with his hands. ''Lessie, I'm sorry...''

''No.'' She backed away until her hips were pressed to the table. ''Don't try that sweet, loving, tender routine. Every time you do that I forget, and let myself slip back into those old feelings. But I don't want to forget, Drew. I want to remember, in order to keep from getting hurt again.''

''I never wanted to hurt you.'' He stepped closer and ran his hands across her shoulders, down her arms, all the while pressing his mouth to a tangle of hair at her temple. ''Leaving you was the hardest thing I've ever done.''

''Then why...?''

''Shhh. Just let me hold you a minute.'' He drew her closer. ''Your grandfather phoned me tonight, Lessie.''

"Why?"

"To say he'd be here first thing in the morning. We'll have our meeting, and then I'll be on my way."

"You're leaving? Tomorrow? And you weren't going to tell me?"

"I thought it best that way." He was brushing soft, butterfly kisses over her forehead, her eyelid, her cheek. "We seem to get a little crazy when we have to say goodbye."

"But I…"

"Shhh. Don't talk. Just let me hold you." He whispered the words against her temple, her cheek, her ear. Words that had her sighing as she struggled to resist the desire to ask for more.

As if reading her mind he traced the outline of her mouth with his tongue, then avoided her mouth, kissing the tip of her nose instead. She couldn't seem to help herself. She pressed closer and shuddered with impatience until his mouth found hers.

This was what she'd been dreading even as she found herself welcoming it. This heat that ebbed and flowed, spreading the most amazing sensations all through her system, to her very core. Tiny darts of pleasure prickled along her spine, pushing aside reason. Taking over her will, until all she wanted was this.

There was hunger in their kiss. A hunger that

drove them to take the kiss deeper, then deeper still. But nothing would fill the need that was growing, gnawing, driving them until they were both trembling with it.

"It's still there." His words, spoken against her mouth, then inside her mouth, left her weak with desire. "This connection between us has never been severed. There's no sense fighting it."

"I know. Oh, Drew. I know." She twined her arms around his neck and clung to him, returning kiss for kiss.

At first, they were so wrapped up in each other they hardly heard the chorus of feminine voices that punctuated the silence of the night. But as the voices grew louder, they lifted their heads and instinctively stepped apart.

"Why, look." Celeste recognized the voice of the moderator from the morning's panel discussion. "Celeste Sullivan. And Drew Hampton. How good to find both of you out here. We've been continuing the fascinating discussion of the price of success. Will you two join us for a drink?"

Drew gallantly deflected the attention away from Celeste, giving her time to compose herself. "Thanks. We already have a drink. But you're welcome to join us."

He indicated the table and chairs and held one for Celeste, who sank into it gratefully. He busied himself snagging several chairs from nearby tables to accommodate the rest of the women.

There was much commotion as the women settled themselves. A waiter was summoned from inside to take their orders. When he returned with a tray of drinks, he held a match to the wick of several hurricane candles and placed them in the center of the table.

With the addition of candlelight the mood lightened and the women began teasing Drew about being the only man in their midst.

He gave a slight bow of his head. "A rose among thorns."

There was a burst of laughter.

"Then be careful what you say," one of them warned with a teasing smile. "Or you might find out just how sharp our thorns can be."

"You needn't worry. I'm no fool." He drained his snifter of brandy, then got to his feet, allowing his hand to linger a moment on Celeste's shoulder. He could feel her tremble beneath his touch. "I believe I'd be wise to leave you ladies alone now. I'm sure you'll be much more comfortable expressing yourselves once I'm gone."

Celeste watched him walk away. And noticed that every woman around the table did the same. And why wouldn't they? It wasn't just his rugged good looks. He was a man who commanded attention, even in a crowd. There was an air of authority about him. A look of success that went much deeper than the superficial. Like Jeremiah, she thought suddenly, Drew was a man completely comfortable with himself and those around him.

She watched that slow, easy walk that reminded her of a lion moving through his kingdom. Without a care in the world.

With an effort she managed to paste a smile to her lips as she forced herself to focus her attention on the women around her.

The women continued their discussion for more than two hours. At first Celeste toyed with the idea of slipping away after a respectable length of time. But in the end she lingered, not only because she felt she was expected to stay, but also because she found herself actually enjoying the lively conversation. These were women who understood the sense of pride that came with their success, and the downside of that same success. She was able to appreciate the hard work that had brought them to this place, and to commiserate with them over the sacrifices still to come.

"I know we're all tired of hearing this, but my biological clock is ticking."

Celeste glanced at the pretty young executive seated across from her who had just voiced the feelings of many of the women around her.

"Unless I have that baby in the next couple of years, time will pass me by."

"And if you do have that baby," remarked another, "can you still keep up the pace necessary to hold on to your job?"

"I think I can. With good daycare or a competent nanny. My mother did it," the young woman said emphatically.

"Was your mother the executive of a busy ad agency?"

The others laughed.

Celeste stared down into the amber liquid in her glass, thinking about her own childhood. What had her grandfather called them? A family of gypsies. A fairly accurate description. They'd barely lingered in any one place for more than a year or two. As soon as their current hotel was operating at a profit, they would move on to take charge of the next failing operation.

And here she was, all those years later, still doing the same thing.

The conversation moved on to other things, but Celeste found herself still lost in thought. Until the untimely arrival of Drew, there had been no doubt in her mind. She'd known exactly what she wanted out of life. And what she wanted was this. Just this.

Now he had her questioning everything she'd always taken for granted.

Damn him.

Was this all there was to her life? Hard work, late nights with guests, and an empty bed at the end of the day? Her choice, of course. But would she be willing to exchange any of this for a husband and family? And why should she? Why couldn't she have it all?

She glanced around at the other women, wondering if they were struggling with the same questions. Even those who'd boasted of being happily married had grudgingly admitted that it came at a high price. They felt as if they were juggling too many balls in the air. They were constantly choosing which one to catch, and which to let drop.

Their problem, Celeste told herself. As for her, she was very good at juggling. She'd had very good teachers.

When, several hours later, their little party began to break up, Celeste made her way to the elevator and punched the button for the top floor. As the doors slid silently open, she found herself hoping that Drew would invite her in for a nightcap. She was too revved to think about sleep.

She smiled to herself. Who was she kidding? It had nothing to do with the fact that she was wide awake, and everything to do with the fact that what she really wanted was to continue that little scene they'd started hours ago in the courtyard. In her present state of mind, it would be very easy for

Drew to persuade her to take it to its logical conclusion.

She paused. Was that what she wanted? To be persuaded? What was happening to her? She was usually so sure of herself. She had never been some sweet, malleable little thing, eager to be talked into a man's bed. Even when she and Drew had become lovers, the choice had been hers. She'd been so sure. So ready for that step. Now she wasn't sure of anything. Except that, in the end, she was the one responsible for her heart. If it got trampled again, she'd have no one to blame but herself.

She paused outside her door and fished for her key, noisily inserting it in the lock. When she heard no sound behind her she glanced over her shoulder to see if Drew had opened his door. She was disgusted to see it firmly closed. There was no light coming from underneath. She felt a wave of annoyance. Had he already gone to sleep?

She crossed the hall and listened at his door. There was no sound coming from inside.

Feeling oddly deflated, she retraced her steps and inserted the key in her lock, letting herself into her darkened suite.

Inside she flipped on the lights and kicked off her shoes before sinking down on the edge of the bed. It was just as well, she told herself. She'd been acting completely out of character ever since Drew had arrived at the Old Liberty Tavern.

It was time to take charge of her life again. She'd always been a woman who knew exactly who she was and where she was going.

The last thing she needed was to get all mushy and sentimental and fall into Drew Hampton's bed for old times' sake.

She undressed and crawled into bed, feeling as though she'd just missed a golden opportunity. And though she told herself it was because she'd been hoping for this one last chance to settle things between them, she knew that was a lie.

She'd wanted to spend this night, Drew's last here in Liberty, in his bed. Wanted, more than any-thing, to feel the way she'd once felt when she'd been thoroughly, completely loved. The way only Drew had ever been able to love her.

Chapter 8

Celeste knew she was taking more time than usual getting herself ready for the day. It couldn't be helped. She had an image in mind that she wanted Drew to carry with him when he left here. That of a polished, successful and contented woman who certainly wouldn't mourn his departure. And why should she? She'd been carrying on for more than a year without him. And doing very well, thank you.

She practiced several smiles in the mirror. All of them looked fake. She sighed and pulled on a pale green jacket over the matching sheath, knowing it flattered her hair and coloring. She added a simple gold chain around her throat before slipping her feet into sensible pumps.

If she paused for several seconds after locking the door to her suite, it wasn't because she was waiting for Drew to step out of his room. Hearing no sound coming from the room across the hall she squared her shoulders and walked to the elevator.

Downstairs she made her way to her office where Daniel O'Malley was cradling a phone to his shoulder while writing furiously. He smiled and waved as she sailed toward her inner office.

Minutes later he knocked and walked to her desk, handing her a list of phone calls and messages. "Mr. Hampton was here earlier."

Her head came up sharply. For a minute she couldn't seem to breathe. "Has he already left?"

Her assistant shook his head. "Not yet. He said if you were down early enough he'd like you to join him for breakfast. But that was more than an hour ago."

Her heart fell. It was his last morning here. Her last chance to talk to him alone. They might have been able to use this time to clear the air between them. And she'd wasted it fussing over her clothes.

Just then there was a sharp rap and Drew poked his head around the open door. In his hands was a linen-covered tray.

Celeste's smile bloomed. "I was afraid I'd missed you."

"No such luck." He strode across the room. "I already had my breakfast." He easily moved aside her paperwork and set the tray in the middle of her desk. "But I thought we could share a last espresso together."

Hearing the phone in the outer office ringing, Daniel stepped back and closed the door, leaving them alone.

"Are you all packed?" Celeste watched as Drew pulled up a chair and settled himself across from her.

He nodded as he reached for the coffee cup and crossed his legs, easing himself back. "My bags are in the car. Now I can relax. No need to rush. I have about an hour before your grandfather's due to arrive."

"Have you decided what you'll recommend to your board?"

He gave her an easy smile. "Yeah."

Seeing that he intended to say nothing more, she busied herself unfolding a napkin and picking up her cup. If this was some sort of contest, she had no intention of being first to blink.

"How did your gab session with your fellow businesswomen go last night?"

"Fine." She forced a brightness to her voice she wasn't feeling. "I'm really glad they happened along. They saved us from…doing something we'd probably be regretting by now.''

''Yeah. You're right.'' He drank his coffee without even tasting it. ''It gave me a chance to have a really good night of sleep before facing that long flight to London.''

They both glanced up at the ringing of her phone.

She snatched it after the first ring, annoyed at the interruption. ''Not now, Daniel.''

She paused, then her face became wreathed with smiles. ''Of course I'll speak with him. Grandpa Sully. Are you in the lobby?'' She glanced at Drew. ''Yes. He's here. All right.'' She pressed a button before returning the receiver to its cradle. ''Go ahead, Grandpa Sully. I have you on the speaker phone.''

''Andrew?'' Patrick Sullivan's brogue boomed over the line. ''Can you hear me?''

Drew grinned. ''Loud and clear, sir. How was your flight?''

''That's what I'm calling about. There's been another delay. I'm sorry to be making such a mess of things. I know you were planning on leaving Liberty today.''

Drew arched a brow and glanced at Celeste. ''Well, I do have a lot of work piling up…''

''Of course you do. But it can't be helped.

Something came up here. I'm going to be tied up for a couple more days.''

"Fine, sir. I'll just fly down to Venice after I take care of a little business in London."

"No, Andrew." The old man's voice sounded surprisingly firm. "I'm afraid I'm going to have to insist that you wait for me there."

Drew sighed and set aside his cup, leaning closer to the phone. "I suppose I could delay my departure if you think it's that important."

"I do, lad. I hope this doesn't inconvenience you too much."

Drew was already glancing at his watch, considering the flight plans that would have to be cancelled, the phone calls he'd have to make, explaining yet another delay. "When do you expect to get in?"

"I can't give you a firm day or time yet. Let me clear the decks with a few things and I'll get back to you." Without a pause for breath the old man continued, "Celeste, my darlin' lass, I look forward to some time alone with you."

"I can't wait to see you, Grandpa Sully. Call me and let me know when to expect you."

"I will, lass. Count on it. Goodbye, Andrew. Celeste."

The line went dead.

Drew drained his cup and set it on the tray, then got to his feet. He couldn't decide if he was happy or annoyed at this latest change of plans. But one thing was certain. It was definitely playing havoc with his heart. The roller coaster had just taken another hill at top speed.

"I'd better get my luggage up to my room. I have some calls to make." He started across the room, then paused as another thought struck. "Would you mind clearing this with your front desk? I'd already checked out."

Celeste nodded.

When he was gone, she steepled her hands and leaned forward, resting her chin on them. Temptation, it seemed, wasn't about to be snatched from her after all. She'd have a few more days to fight the battle she'd been waging since Drew first arrived here.

But now she had something more to worry about, as well. Her grandfather had been so insistent upon meeting with Drew here instead of in Venice. That could only mean he intended to prepare her for the imminent loss of her hotel to the Van Dorn chain.

She stood and began to pace, trying to sort through so many conflicting thoughts. On the one hand, the sale of the tavern would free her to move on to something bigger, more glamorous. Wasn't that what she'd wanted? She paused. She wasn't sure anymore. Always before, the thought of moving on had brought a sense of exhilaration. A feeling of excitement at the coming challenge. But now, suddenly, with the thought looming before her, she felt a wave of sadness. She'd poured so much of herself into this place. Every room bore her signature. Every employee had been personally chosen by her. Except, of course, Jeremiah, who had such a long history with the Old Liberty Tavern, and had become as much a fixture as the ancient clock in the lobby. She would miss him. Miss this place.

She shrugged off her sense of impending loss. She realized that she had work to do. There was no time to brood. She picked up the phone and punched in a number.

Hearing the voice on the other end she said, "Bitsy, there's been a change in Mr. Hampton's plans. He won't be checking out after all." She paused. "No, I don't know his check-out date. Leave that detail open."

She hung up the phone and bent to her paperwork, determined to blot out all thought except the work ahead of her. Work had always been her refuge when she was mulling over troublesome problems.

Drew dialed the phone. While waiting to be put through to the chairman of Van Dorn Hotels he shrugged out of his suit jacket and began tugging off his tie and opening the neck of his shirt. He frowned at the open suitcase, contemplating the thought of unpacking, and later, repacking all those things.

"Mr. Van Dorn."

"Andrew. I didn't expect to hear from you until you arrived in London. Are you already en route?"

"No. Sorry. My plans have changed again." In a few brief words he explained about Patrick Sullivan's unexpected delay, and the opportunity to meet with him face-to-face. "There was no way I could politely refuse. Nor would I want to. I suspect he's prepared to offer us a deal."

"Excellent." The voice on the other end sounded jubilant. "How soon will the two of you meet?"

"I don't know. He said he'd let me know when to expect him. But it might not be for a couple of days."

"You're taking this very well, Andrew. I'm sure it can't be easy to spend so much time in the middle of nowhere. But I want you to know Van Dorn Hotels will never forget this sacrifice you're making for the sake of the company. We value such loyalty."

"Thank you, sir."

"Now land that fish for us, Andrew. You may consider it a minnow, but it could become a whale of an opportunity for Van Dorn Hotels in the U.S."

"Yes, sir." Drew replaced the receiver and sat

back, feeling like a hypocrite. Sacrifice? If that was
true, why was he feeling like a kid who'd just been
given a couple of days off school?

Restless, he booted up his computer and rolled
up his sleeves before reading the dozen or more e-
mails awaiting him, replying to each in turn. Then
he sent off a number of faxes before turning to the
phone messages.

It was several hours before he managed to make
a dent in the paperwork. But, he thought, at least
he wouldn't have to think about packing again for
a couple more days.

He strolled out to the balcony of his room and
caught sight of Celeste down in the courtyard talking to a member of the cleaning crew. She was
gesturing, and the man nodding as she explained
what she wanted him to do.

As she walked away Drew watched her with na-
ked hunger. Alone in his room he didn't have to
put on the game face he showed to the rest of the
world.

He leaned a hip against the railing of the balcony
and crossed his arms over his chest. He didn't
think it was possible to get through a few more
days without getting his hands on her. Just seeing
her made him ache with need.

This had been a big mistake. He knew that now.
Seeing her again had made him realize that he still
wanted her as much as ever. But he had put himself

in an impossible position. If Patrick Sullivan intended to come here to make a deal, he would have to advise the board of Van Dorn Hotels to take it. To do otherwise would be to betray the trust of the company that paid his salary. But by doing that, Celeste would always resent him for taking over something she'd worked so hard to revive.

He'd been put in the unenviable position of being damned if he did; damned if he didn't. And carrying the weight of two corporations on his shoulders.

Jeremiah spotted Drew stepping off the elevator. "Good evening, Mr. Hampton."

Drew smiled. "Jeremiah."

"I haven't seen you around all day." The old man looked at him closely. "Don't tell me you've spent such a beautiful day in your room."

Drew nodded. "I've been letting a lot of paperwork pile up, hoping to handle it back in London. But since I'm not going there just yet, I figured I'd better deal with it."

The old man walked across the lobby beside him. "I heard that your plans had changed yet again. I hope you don't mind being forced to spend a few more days in our little town."

"Not at all, Jeremiah. I can't think of a nicer place to be than right here in Liberty."

The old man paused. "I believe you mean that."

"I do, Jeremiah. This place has completely won me over. It would be easy to lose my heart to the Old Liberty Tavern."

Jeremiah beamed. "I know exactly what you mean, Mr. Hampton. It happened to me a lifetime ago. And though I've been all over the world, this is the place I've always chosen to come back to."

Drew arched a brow. "It seems to me that Celeste mentioned something about you traveling with her grandfather. But I didn't know you'd been all over the world."

"Oh my, yes. Paddy and I used to arrange to meet in India, or Tibet, or on a South Sea island." He chuckled, remembering. "We'd go about looking like common tourists, trying out every hotel around, to see if there was anything worth adding to the Sullivan empire."

"So you and Paddy go back a long way."

"A very long way, sir." He opened the heavy front door for a guest just arriving, carrying a yapping Pekinese in her arms. "Good evening, Mrs. Boudreau. Shall I hold Princess while you check in?"

The woman gave him a dazzling smile. "Thank you, Jeremiah." She handed over the little dog. "Oh, Princess and I have missed you so much. What would we do without the Old Liberty Tavern to visit every now and then?"

She crossed the lobby to the front desk, while

Jeremiah soothed and petted the dog until it fell silent.

The old man glanced over at Drew. "I've enjoyed our little chat, Mr. Hampton, but I'm afraid I'll have to help Mrs. Boudreau settle into her suite now. By the way, Miss Celeste asked you to join her in the courtyard."

"She did?" Drew couldn't hide his surprise. He figured she'd be avoiding him like a plague until after he and her grandfather had concluded their business.

Jeremiah nodded. "The Old Liberty Tavern is hosting a musicale under the stars this evening. I think you'll enjoy it."

When he walked away, Drew continued staring after him. There was a twinkle in the old man's eyes. And a spring to his step. He found himself wondering just what had caused it. Then he shrugged aside the thought. Whether it was the anticipated arrival of Paddy Sullivan, or the presence of the lovely Mrs. Boudreau, mattered not.

He went off in search of Celeste, feeling more than a little pleased that she'd sent for him.

Almost every chair in the courtyard was filled with people tapping their toes to popular show tunes. Right now the band was playing a rollicking song from *The Music Man*.

Waiters moved among the tables, balancing

trays and dispensing drinks. Couples old and young sat entranced by the spell of the music.

Drew glanced around. It was an easy matter to spot Celeste. Her red hair was like a beacon in a sea of brunettes. She stood unobtrusively to one side, careful not to block the view of any of the guests. When one of the waiters brought her a chair, she sat, keeping an eye on the wait staff as they circulated among the guests.

The music changed. Slowed. The haunting notes of "Summertime" drifted on the evening air.

Drew remained in the shadows, studying Celeste. He found it impossible to look away. He loved watching her. The way the breeze caught her hair and lifted it. The way she looked in profile as she studied the crowd. He could almost see the pride in her eyes.

As if sensing him, she turned her head. For the space of a second their gazes met and held. He felt as if all the air had been knocked from his lungs.

Had he imagined that heat? Was he simply seeing things that weren't really there?

The music ended and there was enthusiastic applause. Celeste got to her feet and started toward the door. Drew turned and followed her inside.

She was already halfway across the foyer when he caught up with her. Feeling his hand on her arm she whirled. "You're following me."

"You invited me."

She had her hands on her hips. "I what?"

"Jeremiah told me you wanted me to join you in the courtyard."

"I did?" She paused, thinking back to the last time she'd spoken to Jeremiah. It was true that Drew's name had come up. But she was pretty sure it had been Jeremiah who had done the talking. It was too late in the day. Her mind was too befuddled. She couldn't remember anything too clearly after sixteen hours on her feet. She shrugged. "If I did, I can't remember why."

Drew began walking along beside her. "As long as we're both here, how about some dinner? When's the last time you ate?"

She paused. "I guess I forgot to eat today. I don't think I've had anything since that espresso you brought me this morning."

"There. You see?" His smile was quick, easy. "Time to fuel that body, Ms. Sullivan. Where would you like to eat? Here? Or in town?"

She thought a minute. "What I'd really like to do is get out of these clothes and into something comfortable. Maybe I'll just order up to my room."

"Sounds good. Order enough for two."

She paused at the elevator, shaking her head. "I don't think that's a good idea, Drew."

"All right, then. Let's make it my room." He

stepped inside and punched the button for the top floor.

Celeste was forced to step inside or be left behind. As the doors glided closed he gave her that killer smile.

She looked away. But not before her heart absorbed another blow. She'd probably regret this later. But right at the moment she was feeling weak. And far too tired to argue.

At least that's all she was willing to admit to at the moment. If there was more to this...well, she'd deal with it later.

"All right. My room. Half an hour. If you're late, I won't guarantee there'll be anything left but crumbs."

Chapter 9

At the knock on her door Celeste hurried to open it. She felt a quick sexual tug at the sight of Drew in jeans and a T-shirt. Without the cover of a suit jacket his body seemed even more perfectly sculpted, with wide, muscled shoulders and trim, narrow waist and hips. It was a body she'd once known as intimately as her own.

She glanced at his bare feet. "You forgot your shoes."

"You did say casual." He stepped inside.

She stared pointedly at the ice bucket in his hand. In it were several amber bottles. She wrinkled her nose. "You brought beer?"

"Not just any beer. Wait until you taste this."

"Where did you get it?"

"From your bar downstairs." At her arched look he added, "Yeah. I know. It'll be added to my bill. But it's worth it. You stock an excellent selection."

She laughed. "Of course we do. I told you. I chose every item myself."

"Ah, but have you tasted every one?"

"If I did, I wouldn't be able to get any work done. I'd be perpetually drunk."

"Which might not be all bad." He leaned close and watched as she stepped back a pace. "At least you'd be relaxed for a change."

"Relaxed? I'd be unconscious."

He set the bucket on the bar and uncapped two bottles, pouring one into a glass for her. "Try this."

She tasted. Paused. Considered. "It's...different."

"Yeah. But do you like it?"

She sipped again. Swallowed. Then nodded. "It's really smooth. Very light." She nodded. "I like it a lot."

He smiled. "I thought you would. It's a new German import." Taking a pull from the bottle he looked around. "This is nice. It looks like you."

"Thanks. I haven't had much time to decorate. I wanted to concentrate on the rest of the inn, so I've kept my space simple."

"Simple?" He smiled as he wandered the room that looked as if it had been professionally decorated down to the smallest detail. "I remember these. Your grandmother's crystal candlesticks."

Celeste nodded. "I like looking at them. I've always been so glad she wanted me to have them."

He stood back to study the art on the walls. A pleasing mix of soft watercolors and bold contemporaries. There was even a European country scene by an artist who commanded a fortune for his work. "You've added to your collection."

She laughed softly. "You're the only one who would notice. Do you like it?"

"Yeah. And I like this." He touched a hand to the bronze bust of a little girl resting atop a carved Oriental chest.

"My mother gave it to me. She said I ought to have it, since I was the model when she cast it about twenty-five years ago."

He studied it more carefully before lifting his head. "Now that you've said that, I recognize those laughing eyes and that stubborn little chin."

"Not to mention the Sullivan nose," she said with a laugh.

He caught her chin and studied her profile. And had to absorb a quick flash of heat for his effort. "I've always liked that turned-up nose."

"Even when I stick it in someone else's business?"

"Absolutely." He bent close and rubbed the tip of his nose over hers. "As long as it's not my business."

He stepped back and gave her an admiring look that had the heat rising to her cheeks. "I've been meaning to tell you. I like your idea of casual."

She was wearing yellow shorts and a stretchy little cropped top in pale lemon yellow. He found the drape of the fabric extremely sexy, especially since it seemed to emphasize every line and curve of her body. On her feet were matching sandals. He glanced down at her carefully manicured bare toes peeking out. "Do you remember the time I gave you a pedicure?"

"Umm." She pursed her lips. How could she forget? He'd done it on a dare. And it had turned into one of the most purely sensual things they'd ever done, outside of making love. She shivered, still able to recall the feel of his hands on her toes, her feet, her legs.

She knew he was remembering, too. It was impossible to ignore the wolfish look on his face. She was grateful for the knock on the door.

She turned away a little too quickly. "Here's our dinner."

"And just in time, wouldn't you say?"

She laughed, knowing he'd been much too aware of her discomfort. "Yes. I would."

She hurried over to hold the door while a waiter wheeled in a serving cart.

"Good evening, Ms. Sullivan. Mr. Hampton."

"Hello, Billy." Celeste greeted him with a warm smile. "You can just wheel it over to the French doors and leave it. We'll serve ourselves."

Drew handed him a tip as he was leaving. When he turned Celeste was already removing covered trays and carrying them to a small glass table on the balcony.

Drew stepped out and breathed in the warm night air. Unlike his balcony that overlooked the courtyard, hers had a view of the entire town of Liberty. Colorful roofs and church spires looked postcard perfect in the moonlight. Streetlights spilled warm yellow puddles into the darkness. Lights in windows winked and flickered, making it look, from this vantage point, like a fairy-tale village.

"This is wonderful." He topped off her glass, before opening a second bottle for himself. He stood at the railing and studied the scene. "I can see why you love it here."

"Can you?" Her eyes glowed in the light of the hurricane candles as she held a match to them before replacing the domes.

"Yeah." He watched her step closer until she was standing beside him.

Her voice was hushed as she looked at the scene

spread before them. "I've tried to explain it to my parents, but they just don't understand."

He turned to her, leaning a hip against the railing. "Have they been here?"

She nodded. "And they declared it a lovely, quaint little place. But I could see that they had no idea why I would ever want to spend any more time here than necessary."

"And do you? Want to spend more time here?"

"I...don't know what I want. I've been here a year. That ought to be enough. But I have the feeling that the Old Liberty Tavern hasn't even come close to its potential yet. I just keep thinking that there's so much more that could be done here."

He studied her eyes, seeing a wistful look in them. "How about your grandfather? What does he think?"

She shrugged. "Grandpa Sully understands. He's always had a special fondness for New Hampshire. Even though he spends most of his time in Europe, he always used to come here once a year to get away from the business."

"Yeah." Drew nodded. "The fishing lodge at Snug Harbor. I've been there."

"I'd forgotten that." She looked up to see him watching her. "You and Grandpa Sully flew there shortly before you left to join Van Dorn." There it was again. That quick flash of pain at the memory of his abrupt departure from the company and from her life. "Anyway, it was Grandpa Sully who suggested I come here and try to, as he called it, weave my magic on this poor failing little place."

"A smart man, your grandfather. And he was right to call it magic. I've had a chance to review the before-and-after profit-and-loss statements. No one but a magician could have saved this failing old tavern. You've done an amazing job here."

She flushed with pleasure at his words. But then, she'd always loved the fact that he shared her love of, and pride in, the business of innkeeping. It was a bond she'd never been able to share with any other man.

Seeing the way she paused, staring into the distance, he inclined his head toward the covered tray. "Are you going to feed me or just torment me with that mouth-watering smell of grilled onions?"

She laughed. "If I weren't so hungry, I'd make you wait until you were begging. But the truth is, I can't stand waiting either. Come on."

He took a seat and she lifted the lid to reveal two huge, perfectly broiled hamburgers still sizzling on a heated tray, and smothered in mushrooms, onions and green pepper.

Drew arched a brow. "Do you think they're big enough?"

She couldn't help laughing harder. "I guess Marcus thought we'd be starving."

"Either that, or you told him you wanted burgers as big as Rhode Island."

She lifted another lid to reveal a plate heaped with thick steak fries. "I believe I'm going to see that Marcus gets a bonus in his next paycheck."

"A fine idea." Drew helped himself to a fry and closed his eyes. "The man is a kitchen god."

"I thought you might approve. I figure, with all that around-the-world traveling you do, you probably yearn for some good old American food now and then."

"You know me a little too well."

Again that flush before she took a bite of her burger. She gave a sigh of pleasure. "Oh, this may be worth a double bonus to Marcus."

Seeing the way she was enjoying her food, Drew followed suit.

"This may be," he said between bites, "the best burger I've ever tasted."

"Are you often given to these little bouts of exaggeration?"

"Not often." He polished off several more fries and washed them down with beer. "How's yours? Just average?"

"Quiet." She chewed, swallowed, then whispered, "I'm about to go into rapture."

They were both grinning like fools as they devoured the rest of their meal, then sat back sipping beer.

"I could learn to love this." Drew stretched out his long legs and looked out over the sleepy little town.

"It is peaceful, isn't it?" Celeste tucked her feet up under her and leaned back, breathing in the soft summer scents.

Drew took the time to look around. Even this small balcony bore the distinct imprint of Celeste's exquisite taste. A huge pot of white roses stood in one corner, twining their way up a lovely old trellis attached to the brick wall. Colorful planters of pink petunias and trailing ivy sat atop the railing. A statue of a girl holding a bird in her hands was actually a small fountain. The sound of running water was a soothing balm.

Out in the courtyard the musicians started another set of show tunes. The muted notes drifted upward to mingle with the sound of softly falling water.

Drew gave her a long, contemplative look. "You've made a fabulous home for yourself here."

"Thanks."

"Tell me about the winter. Were you buried in snow?"

She laughed. "You know that little village in the Alps where we went skiing?"

He nodded.

"It can't hold a candle to the snow around here."

"Did you find time to ski?"

"Not often. But I did a little skiing. We have some pretty impressive runs on the mountain."

He smiled. "I heard you describing the setting to that young couple getting married. It sounded like paradise. I was trying to picture myself sipping hot mulled wine by an open fire, and watching skaters out on the pond. That was quite a scene you painted."

Suddenly restless under his gaze, Celeste uncoiled from the chair. "Coffee?"

"Sure." He stood. "I'll get the cups if you'll tell me where you keep them."

They stepped inside and she pointed toward a cupboard. "Up there."

He retrieved cups and saucers while she filled a carafe and carried it to the table. While she poured, he began humming to the music of "Some Enchanted Evening."

When she turned he was standing in front of her, arms open wide. "May I have this dance, miss?"

With a laugh she stepped closer and began to move with him. She knew at once it was a mistake, but there seemed no graceful way to step back. Those strong arms were already gathering her against him. Her body was already reacting to his. As his arms tightened around her she felt an old familiar ache. When he pressed his lips to her temple she felt heat begin to build, a slow, pulsing tide through her veins. And then they were moving in the dance, their bodies barely brushing.

"We were always good together, Lessie." The words, spoken against her cheek, sent sparks dancing along her spine.

He knew just how to soften her up. The use of that nickname did things to her heart that she was unable to control. "We were always too good, Drew. That was the problem."

He looked down at her. "I don't recall it ever being a problem."

"Then you have a...selective memory." She struggled to ignore the warmth of his breath whispering across her face. "Every time we came together we set off fireworks."

He shot her a devilish grin. "Are you saying that's wrong?"

"Of course not. But instead of...going up in flames, we should have been cooling things down. Talking more. Sharing our minds along with our bodies."

"Oh. I see. It's my mind you really wanted." The corners of his lips curved, though he tried not to laugh. "And all this time I thought it was my body that turned you on."

"I love your body, Drew. You know I always have."

"That's a relief. I'd hate to find out that you'd been faking it. Especially since…" He stopped swaying to the music as he lowered his face to hers. "…I've never been able to forget about yours."

"Drew. Don't…"

He swallowed her protest with a kiss so hot, so hungry, they were both rocked by it.

She'd thought she could resist. She'd prepared herself for every possibility. The sweet words. The burning looks. The sizzling touches. But the moment his mouth covered hers, she was swamped by so many emotions, she felt helpless to fight.

Until now she'd been able to feel him holding back. Reluctant to take her where she didn't choose to go. Giving her time to step back. But this time was different. He poured everything into this kiss. A kiss that drained her even while it filled her. A kiss that demanded all, and then even more, until there was nothing more to give. A kiss that was bold, possessive, and at the same time so generous. So giving. So like Drew, it made her want to weep.

He took the kiss deeper. It spoke of such deep hunger. Of a need so wild, so primitive, it frightened her.

She couldn't breathe. Couldn't think. All she could do was hold on as his mouth plundered hers. She absorbed a series of quick jittery jolts to the system as his mouth began to move almost savagely over hers.

Hadn't she known this would happen if they were alone? Yet, even knowing, she'd invited him in. Had foolishly opened the door to the wolf waiting to devour her.

Because she'd wanted this as much as he did. There was no denying the truth. From the moment she'd seen Drew Hampton that first morning in her office, she'd wanted this. And everything leading up to this moment had merely been a dance. A lover's dance, designed to soothe the fears, calm the nerves and leave her without defenses when he finally stormed the gates.

She sighed as he changed the angle of the kiss. She could feel her blood heating by degrees, her bones melting. Could feel her heartbeat pounding in her temples. Could feel her breathing growing more ragged, as his hands, those big, clever hands that knew her body so intimately, began moving over her.

She was so tired of fighting. Wasn't this what they both wanted? Still, somewhere in the back of her mind was that nagging voice of reason. They'd traveled this path before, and it had ended in disaster. She'd given in to the demands of her heart, only to have it trampled and left in the dust. How many times did she have to be hurt before she learned her lesson?

"Drew. Wait."

He was almost beyond hearing. His blood was so hot he could feel himself close to meltdown. The need for her was so great he was trembling. "I don't think I can wait any longer." He ran hot wet kisses down her throat.

"Listen to me." She pushed ineffectively against his chest, but all that did was inflame him more. "We need to think, Drew."

"I'm tired of thinking. Come on, Lessie. Let's just do what feels good. You know you want this, too." He plunged his hands into her hair and tipped her face up for his kiss.

"I do. That's the trouble."

He heard the slight change in her voice and recognized it. She was close to tears. He felt the slight trembling of her lips on his and drew back.

His eyes narrowed on hers. "If you want what I want, what's the problem?"

"Us, Drew. We're the problem. We've already been through this. And it solved nothing. I don't think I could go through it again. I couldn't bear to make love with you tonight and say goodbye to you tomorrow."

"That's the way our lives are. In fact, you told me a thousand times or more that you didn't want to put down roots. You'd feel hemmed in by tradition. It was you who wanted the freedom to wander the world. To taste every food, drink every wine, learn every language and live your life exactly as your parents and grandparents had. Without strings, you said. You told me you liked it that way, Lessie.''

"I did like things that way once upon a time." She couldn't stop the trembling in her voice. "But I…don't know anymore. Help me here, Drew. Help me think this through."

"Sorry. I don't do my best thinking when I'm holding you in my arms." He gave a shaky laugh and touched a fingertip to her face. Just a touch, before lowering his hand to his side. "Hell, I don't know the answer. I quit trying to figure things out a long time ago. I've given up on thinking. All it does is make things worse."

He took a step back and she felt a sudden chill. "You know what I want, Lessie. You. Just you. That's never changed. But maybe I'm not enough for you. Maybe I never was. If that's the case, it's better to say so now. It'll hurt. But then, we've hurt each other before. I'll leave it up to you. The choice has to be yours."

She closed her eyes against the pain. She wanted, more than anything, to beg him to take her. Here. Now. Before she had time to think. To reason. To remember. To resist. But wasn't that what she always did? Pick things apart until she'd reasoned them to death?

In the silence that followed he nodded before muttering, "I see."

Just two words. But there was such finality in them. His eyes went flat. As flat as the tone of his voice, before he turned away.

Celeste watched as he crossed the balcony and stepped through the open doorway into her room. She felt as if she were choking. Her throat was clogged with unshed tears. She ran a tongue over her lips, wondering if she could manage a single word.

"Drew." She swallowed. Tried again. "Wait."

He never heard her as he stalked across the room and tore open the door to her room. She watched as he walked out and slammed the door behind him.

The sound seemed to reverberate through her suite, blotting out the music. Blotting out even the sound of the fountain, until all she could hear was the echo of the slamming door. And his footsteps as he crossed to his own room.

And then the only sound was her breathing, shallow and uneven, as she struggled not to give in to the tears that threatened.

Chapter 10

Drew walked across the room running his hands wearily over his face. How many times did he have to be stabbed in the heart before he learned his lesson? What had he been thinking, coming to Liberty like a lovesick fool? It may have started out as strictly business, but he'd begun to foster the belief that once Celeste saw him again, she would remember what they'd once had, and try to rekindle that old flame.

He'd forgotten what a hardheaded little realist she was. No soft lights and gentle seductions for Celeste Sullivan. She was on a mission to save the Sullivan empire. Single-handedly if necessary. There was no time for distractions. Certainly no time for love. She was a no-nonsense, down-to-business, thoroughly modern woman. It was something he'd always found so enticing about her. But right now he was fed up with ambition and corporate politics.

The music drifting up from the courtyard was louder in his room, and he swore as he hurried over to draw the balcony door shut. It didn't help. He could still hear the strains of a haunting love song mocking him.

Was that all they knew? Love songs? He ran his hand through his hair and reached for the cord to draw the draperies. He didn't want to see the stars, or the twinkling lights, or the happy people below. Before he could close them, he heard a sharp rap on the door and released the cord.

He stormed across the room and tore open the door, ready to throttle the intruder. "I didn't order any…" His eyes, hot and fierce, narrowed on Celeste. His gaze raked her. "Now what? Didn't you plunge the knife deep enough? Or did you think it might be fun to twist it, too?"

"Oh, Drew." Her voice was strangled with unshed tears. "Don't make this any worse for me."

"For you?" He leaned against the wall and crossed his arms over his chest, taking in the way she looked, her eyes troubled, her lips trembling. For a moment he was almost tempted to comfort her. But only for a moment.

"May..." She glanced around. "May I come in?"

He shifted away from the door, leaving the choice to her. She stepped inside and closed his door, then leaned warily against it while he continued watching her.

"I don't know how to handle this, Drew."

"Handle what?"

"You. Us." She looked absolutely miserable as she shook her head, sending hair tumbling over one eye. "I've always been so focused. Always known exactly what I wanted, and how to get it."

She saw the grin that touched the corner of his lips.

"Oh yeah. I've noticed."

"You know I've never been afraid of hard work, Drew. In fact, I thrive on it. But this... You... Us..." She lifted her hands, then clenched them at her sides, staring at the floor. "Ever since you came here, I've been lost. I don't seem to know where I'm going, or why."

"Join the crowd."

At his terse words she looked up. "You, too?"

"Yeah."

"I didn't realize. You always seem so cool and controlled." She stared into his eyes and could see his pain. Pain she'd inflicted. It cut to the quick. "I'm sorry, Drew."

He shrugged. "I guess you figure I deserve it after leaving you and the company behind."

"No." She touched a hand to his arm. Just a touch, but she felt his muscles tighten. Felt him flinch. "This isn't about revenge, Drew. I'm just so confused. You know how I need to analyze everything. Look at a problem from every angle, before making an informed decision. I've always hated making mistakes. And I'm so afraid that we're going to let our...hunger for each other get in the way of our common sense."

He looked down at her hand, resting lightly on his skin, and felt the heat starting to hum and pulse through his veins. A dangerous thing, he knew.

"Are you saying this...hunger isn't just one-sided? That I'm not alone in wanting this?"

"I've never stopped wanting you, Drew."

"But...?" He shrugged aside the tiny spark of hope that flickered for just a moment in the darkness of his mind. "I'm sure there's a qualifier in there somewhere."

Her voice trembled slightly. "But I'm afraid."

"You have a right to be, Lessie."

Just the sound of that name on his lips had her melting. She wished he would do more to persuade her. She longed to have him touch her, hold her, kiss her. But when he continued standing so still, watching her so carefully, she realized that it was up to her this time.

"When you left just now, I recognized another feeling, even stronger than fear."

"What's that?"

She lifted her hand to his cheek and felt him react as though she'd slapped him. "I want you to hold me, Drew. The way you used to."

"Sorry." He knew his tone was abrupt, but it was taking all his strength to hold himself in check. "That isn't possible. If I hold you now, I won't be able to stop."

She lifted both hands to his chest. "Maybe this time I won't ask you to stop."

He closed his fingers around her wrists, halting her movements. "Nothing's changed since I left your room, Lessie. I'm the same man I was before. You're the same woman. I can't make you any promises that will change things."

"Then I won't ask for any." She stood facing him, her heart in her eyes. "Hold me, Drew. Kiss me. For old times' sake."

She saw the heat flare in his eyes. "If I do, it'll be all the way. Otherwise we stop this right now. We go our separate ways and settle for nothing. Understood?"

She could feel the tension humming through him. Still, he stood his ground.

She found his control unbearably arousing. "I understand."

He shook his head. "I don't think you do, Lessie." He released her wrists to run his hands up her arms, across her shoulders. Every touch of her was pure heaven. And pure hell. "I won't be content with a quick tumble in the sheets."

A little thrill of anticipation raced along her spine. She'd never been able to forget the way he made her feel with a single touch, a single kiss. Like she was the only woman in the world.

"I'll want all of you. Your body, your mind." He pressed his face to her hair. "The way it used to be. And more, Lessie. The way it never was before."

She felt a sudden rush of fear at his words. But just as quickly the fear was replaced by the keen edge of excitement as his lips began moving across her face, burning a trail of kisses from her brow to her cheek, and then to her mouth.

Instead of kissing her, he traced his tongue around the outline of her lips, until she thought she'd go mad with the need to kiss him.

"Drew…" She tried to capture his mouth, but he kept it just out of reach, while his hands pressed her closer and closer against him, until she could feel the imprint of his hard body on hers.

"Tell me, Lessie. Tell me this is exactly what you want, too."

"It is." The words came out in a sigh of desperation. "I'm afraid. Afraid we'll hurt each other again. But I'm even more afraid of letting you go without this last chance. Do you understand?''

"Completely."

At last he covered her mouth with his and kissed her until they were both breathless. Then he kissed her again, this time lingering over her lips, loving the feel of them. Savoring the taste, the texture, the softness. Filling himself with her sweetness.

His head was already spinning. "In all the time we've been apart, I've been torturing myself with thoughts of this." He whispered the words against her mouth. "Of touching you. All of you. Of kissing you until the taste of you filled all my senses and pushed aside everything else. Everything but you."

She was struggling to keep her balance. Her world seemed to have tilted at a crazy angle. She wrapped her arms around his waist and held on. "It's been the same for me. I used to wake up, dreaming of your arms holding me. And find myself weeping when I saw that my bed was empty."

He traced the shape of her ear, before tugging lightly on her lobe, sending darts of pleasure to her very core.

Against her ear he growled, "Some nights I swore I could smell you on my pillow. That perfume you've always worn would be there, taunting me. And I'd lie awake, praying for dawn, so I could lose myself in my work. When all along, all

I really wanted was to lose myself in you.'' He plunged his tongue into her ear, and heard her little hiss of pleasure. ''All I've ever wanted was you. And this. Just this.''

He ran wet, nibbling kisses across her jaw, down her throat, lingering over the sensitive little hollow between her neck and shoulder. The fragrance of her perfume was stronger here, and he could see, in his mind's eye, the way she always touched the stopper to her throat, and then lower, between her breasts.

''I have to see you. All of you.'' Annoyed with the barriers between them, he tugged the cropped top over her head. He wasn't surprised to find silk underneath. It was one of her little indulgences. She'd always loved the feel of silk against her skin.

To him it was just one more barrier to eliminate. He stripped it aside in one quick move.

''Ah, Lessie. You're so beautiful.'' His voice was gruff with emotion.

In the moonlight her milk-white skin seemed touched with gold. Against his fingertips it seemed even softer than the silk he'd just discarded. Almost reverently he trailed his fingers across the soft swell of her breasts, allowing his mouth to follow the trail until she sucked in a breath and held on to keep from falling.

He dipped a finger beneath the waistband of her

soft silky shorts and tugged them free, until they joined the rest of her clothes at their feet.

He loved looking at her. At all that perfect, gilded skin and that mane of fiery hair. And those cool green eyes. At the moment they weren't cool at all, but wide and troubled. Fear of what they were about to do had them even wider than usual, and the knowledge made him even bolder as he kissed her, long and slow and deep, hoping to put her fears at rest.

With a sigh of impatience she tugged his T-shirt over her head and discarded it, then reached for the snaps at his waist. She was frantic to get her hands on him. She needed to feel his body against hers. That beautiful, sculpted body, rippling with muscles. To feel it pressed to hers. Warm flesh to warm flesh.

He'd barely stepped out of his jeans before she was running her palms over the smooth, flat planes of his stomach, then higher, feeling the brush of dark hair against her fingertips. With a little hum of pleasure she followed with her mouth, trailing hot wet kisses across his chest.

He hadn't expected the need to be so desperate. The desire to be so deep. With an oath he dragged her against him and savaged her with kisses.

Her breath was burning her throat. She felt her knees buckle and reached out wildly.

His arm was there, strong and firm. "Don't worry, Lessie. I won't let you fall."

"I never doubted it, Drew."

He found her, hot and moist, and took her on a fast, dizzying climb. He could feel the little tremors that rocked her as she reached the first peak. But before she could recover he was taking her up again. And then again. Leaving her no time to breathe. To steady herself.

"Drew." She stared into those hot, fierce eyes, stunned by the darkness she could see.

"I warned you, Lessie. Not just the way it used to be, but the way it never was. This time, I want to take you places you've never been before."

She felt a sudden shock as she realized that, though they'd been lovers, and had known each other as intimately as lovers could, this was a side of Drew she'd never seen before. This dark, dangerous stranger excited her, even while he frightened her. What surprised her even more was the eager way she responded to him.

He pressed her back against the wall and kissed her until she was weak and clinging. But with each kiss she could feel her own passion growing until she clutched at him and returned his kisses until she could barely breathe.

The heat rose up between them, clogging their throats, leaving their skin damp with sweat. The hot summer air seemed to have closed in around them until there seemed no relief for it. And still they took each other higher.

She'd never known such desperation. She wanted him. Wanted to crawl inside his skin. And yet she was helpless to end this hunger. A hunger that he continued to feed, while slowly driving her mad.

If it weren't for his hands holding her, and his body pressing her to the wall, she knew she'd slip bonelessly to the floor.

She was almost grateful when he dropped to his knees and tugged her down beside him. She twined her arms around his neck, willing to go wherever he led her, the need for him growing with every kiss.

With a growl of pleasure he laid her down and cradled her in his arms, kissing her, touching her as no one else ever had.

"Please, Drew." Her words were a fierce whisper against his mouth, begging him to end this sweetest of tortures.

Instead he slowed his movements, lingering over every kiss, every touch, drawing out each pleasure. He circled her breast with his tongue, then took the already erect nipple into his mouth and suckled until she writhed beneath him, mad with need. He moved to the other breast, nibbling, suckling, teasing until the pleasure was almost pain. And still he held back, keeping relief just out of reach.

He thought of all the endless days and nights he'd dreamed of this. Of lying here with her, loving her, bringing them both pleasure beyond their wildest dreams. But none of his fantasies had ever compared with this. The reality was so much sweeter than anything his imagination could conjure. He studied the way she looked, with moonlight spilling through the balcony window, bathing her in a golden glow. Her hair like fire against his skin. Her eyes, hot as emeralds, staring into his.

It excited him to know that she was as close to madness as he was at this moment. The kiss she begged for was his. His was the touch that left her weak.

It was his name on her lips as she sighed and dragged his head down for another drugging kiss.

The desire to take her, to end this terrible longing, nearly pushed him to the brink. Still he held back, tempting them both as they edged closer and closer to madness.

She sobbed and reached for him. This time he knew he could wait no longer. As he entered her he found himself murmuring words he'd never spoken before. Words of endearment. Words of love. Words straight from the heart.

"I love you, Lessie. I've always loved you. Only you."

Through a blinding mist of passion she heard him. Her vision blurred and she struggled to focus on him. But all she could see were his eyes, hot and fierce, burning into hers. All she could hear was the pounding of her ragged heartbeat, like thunder in her ears.

"Drew." His name was torn from her lips as she shuddered and reached for him.

She'd never known such strength before. Or such deep arousal. She wrapped herself around him, moving with him, climbing with him as they began to soar. Higher, then higher still. Until they seemed to touch the moon. There they exploded into a burst of blinding light. And drifted slowly to earth in a shower of glittering stardust.

Chapter 11

"You okay?" Spent, Drew lay on top of her, his mouth pressed to a tangle of hair at her temple. It felt so good. So right to be here, locked in her arms. As if, he thought, he'd come home.

She nodded, unable to speak. She was mortified to feel tears threatening again. She hadn't cried this much in the year they'd been apart.

Seeing her reaction he was filled with remorse. "I never meant this, Lessie. I never meant to take you on the floor like a savage. The bed…"

She touched a finger to his lips to stop his protest. "I didn't need a bed."

"I'm a brute. I know I'm too heavy…"

"You're not too heavy. And it isn't the floor.

It's just..." She drew in a long, shaky breath. "I've missed you so much, Drew. So much."

"Not as much as I've missed you." He rolled to one side and drew her into the circle of his arms, then lifted her atop him, cushioning her body against his. Her hair swirled forward like a fiery veil, tickling his chest.

"There hasn't been a day that I haven't thought of you, and wondered how you were. You'll never know how many times I went to the phone and dialed your number, then called myself every sort of fool before hanging up."

She traced the curve of his brow. She'd always loved his face. This strong chiseled profile. The rugged features, softened by that smiling poet's mouth. Those gray, mysterious eyes, hiding so many secrets.

"I did the same. A hundred times or more."

"Too bad we never connected."

She gave a wry smile. "What could we have possibly said? Hi. Having a wonderful time. Wish you were here."

At her wistful tone he kissed the tip of her nose. "That's probably what we would have said to cover our true feelings. In fact, the higher up the corporate ladder I climbed, the more I realized I wasn't having a wonderful time at all."

"Neither was I." She sighed. "I plunged myself into so much work, I used to fall into bed every night completely exhausted. But all the work in the world couldn't keep me from thinking about you, and wondering how you were doing.''

''Then you're not sorry…'' He glanced at their clothes, strewn around the room like rags. ''…that we came back to this?''

She shook her head. ''I don't know how I'll feel in the cold light of morning. But right now…'' She wrapped her arms around his neck and lowered her head for a long, slow kiss that started the familiar heat curling deep inside. ''…I'm so glad I found the courage to come after you.''

''Yeah. Me, too.'' He chuckled against her lips. ''I wasn't going to come back and beg again.''

''Is that what you were doing? Begging? And here I thought you'd come back in triumph.''

''Some triumph,'' he whispered against her lips and was jolted by the sudden rush. She was like a drug. One taste and he had to have more.

He drew her down for another long lazy kiss until his head was spinning. Then, for good measure, he rolled them both over and began nibbling his way down her throat to her collarbone, then lower, to the swell of her breast.

When he came up for air he was fully aroused. ''Sorry, but I have a lot of time to make up for. I think we're going to have to try for seconds.'' He nodded toward the bed. ''What say I carry you to someplace more comfortable?''

"It's too far." She sighed and moved against him, brushing her mouth across his chest until he moaned. "We both have a lot of time to make up for. Starting right now. And I don't want to waste a second of it moving from this spot."

He plunged his hands into her hair and drew her head back. "We always did think alike, didn't we?" He ran his lips over hers and nearly devoured her with rough kisses.

They came together with such heat, they were both gasping for air as they rolled across the floor, taking each other on a fast, bruising ride.

Celeste sat up in bed, trying to remember how she'd come to be here. Then she remembered Drew carrying her into the bedroom, kissing her oh-so-softly before depositing her among the bed linens of his king-size bed.

The layout of this suite was identical to hers across the hall. Both the bedroom and the parlor area had balconies that seemed to bring the outdoors inside. The partially opened curtains billowed in on a perfumed summer breeze.

She heard the door open and close. Saw him walking toward the bed.

"Where did you go?"

He crossed the room and handed her a glass. "I went in search of champagne and came up empty, so I went to your suite and brought back the beer."

''Oh.'' She sipped. ''That tastes good.'' She passed the glass back to him to share. ''How did you get in?''

''I helped myself to your key.'' He wiggled his dark brows menacingly. ''It's an old trick I picked up in my days as a secret service agent.''

''In your dreams.''

''Well, in some of them. Though I have to admit you were in most of my dreams. As my sexy partner in crime.'' He held up a plate. ''And I thought, since I was already in your suite without permission, I'd nuke the last of the steak fries.'' He offered her a bite.

''Umm.'' She popped one in her mouth. ''They're every bit as good the second time around.''

''Sort of like us.''

They both laughed.

It was well past midnight, and the musicians downstairs were playing their last set. The music from *Phantom of the Opera* drifted through the doors of the balcony.

Celeste slipped out of bed and threw open the French doors, humming to the music. Absently she picked up his T-shirt and pulled it over her head.

He grinned at her. ''If you're doing that for modesty's sake, it isn't working.''

She glanced down at herself, seeing the way every line and curve was emphasized.

"Good." She walked closer, aware of the way he was watching her as she sat on the edge of the bed facing him. "I'd hate to think you could get me out of your system so easily."

He cupped her face with his hand and brushed a kiss over her lips. "I've never been able to get you out of my system. And I'm not quite sure I ever will."

"Even better." She absorbed the quick little thrill as his hand came to rest possessively on the small of her back, before he drew her close.

"Careful. You wouldn't want to spill beer in your bed."

He set the glass aside and nuzzled her lips. "I can drink imported beer any time. I'd much rather spend my time kissing you."

She leaned into him, loving the way the heat of his touch seemed to spread through her veins and do strange things to her system.

"Umm. Lessie," he muttered against her mouth. "Did I just smash your fingers under my hip?"

She kept her mouth on his while tapping her fingers on his chest. "Both my hands are right here. Why?"

A chuckle started from deep inside and rumbled upward. "Then I guess that must be the plate of fries I just crushed."

"Oh, no." She leaned up to look him in the eye.

"You realize, don't you, that's all the food we had left from dinner?"

"What's the matter?" He grinned. "Afraid you'll starve?"

She shrugged. "It's a long time until breakfast."

"Don't worry." He reached down and removed the plate of ruined fries, setting them on the night table with the beer. Then he hauled her into bed and rolled over her. In one smooth motion he stripped away the T-shirt she was wearing.

Against her throat he whispered, "We'll never starve as long as we have all this loving to feed on."

She had no chance to respond. His kiss, his touch, were already taking her to a place where no words were needed.

"Have you ever been back to Rome?" Celeste was sitting in bed, pillows mounded behind her back, watching through the open bedroom door as Drew rummaged through the tiny refrigerator.

The clock on the bedside table read three. The sky outside the windows was black velvet, sprinkled with millions of diamond stars. A half-moon the color of pure gold made a splash of color.

They'd both awakened at the same time, as if by design, feeling ravenous.

"I had no desire to see Rome alone. I figured it wouldn't be the same without you." He looked up from the sandwich he was making. "How about you?"

She shook her head. "I've never been back." She sank into the pillows, remembering. "I've never known a time like that."

It had been like a wonderful, fanciful fairy tale. A slice of time suspended from reality. They'd laughed, loved, played. And afterward, whenever they felt the pressures of their work, they would remind one another of that special time. It never failed to make them smile.

"Neither have I." He crossed to the bed and climbed in beside her, setting the plate between them.

"What's this?"

"My own creation. I'm calling it the whatever-I-can-find-in-the-refrigerator-that's-edible sandwich."

"Um-hmm." She eyed it suspiciously. "Just what did you find in the refrigerator that's edible?"

"Some cheese. Some lettuce. Half a banana. A little peanut butter. Some mayo." He picked up half and held it to her mouth. "Go ahead. Try it."

"You first."

He rolled his eyes. "What's the matter? Afraid of a little food poisoning?"

"Something like that. Go on, coward. Take the first bite. If you're still around in half an hour, maybe I'll join you."

"If I let you. This may be so delicious, I won't leave any for you but the crumbs." He bit into it and chewed, making little sounds of pleasure as he swallowed.

She was watching him carefully. "Was it really good?"

"Amazing."

She fixed him with a look. "You wouldn't be trying an old con game to sucker me, would you?"

He gave her a mock pained expression. "I'll try to overlook that remark and blame it on your extreme hunger."

She sighed. "All right. I'll try it."

He held it to her lips and she took a small bite and began chewing. When she'd managed to swallow it she smiled. "It really is good. I think I'll have another bite."

"I don't know." He snatched it away. "What are you contributing to this feast?"

She thought a moment. Then she brightened. "In my pantry across the hall I have a tea chest filled with some of the best herbal teas you'll ever taste."

He considered, then said, "What else?"

"Hmm." She smiled. "Also in my pantry is a very good bottle of Merlot. If you're interested."

"Now you've hooked me." He caught her hand and helped her out of bed. "Come on. We may as well bring the tea and the wine."

While she pulled on his hotel robe and searched for her key, he slipped into his jeans. Leaving the waist unsnapped he padded barefoot to the door and followed her across the hall. Minutes later they returned to his room with their bounty, laughing and whispering like two conspirators.

He uncorked the wine and filled two glasses while she opened a paper bag.

He eyed it. "What's that?"

"Oh, something special I found in the pantry while I was hunting up the tea."

He peered over her shoulder, then groaned. "Twinkies? Oh, you know how I love them."

"Uh-huh." She dangled one in front of him. "I figured I'd share these if you'd share that special sandwich."

"Deal."

He made a grab for it, but she held it just out of reach. "Just one more thing."

He waited.

"As soon as we've fortified ourselves, I'd like you to do that...kissing thing you've been doing so well for the past few hours."

His grin was quick and dangerous. "Oh. That kissing thing. That's a specialty of mine, you know. You like that, do you?"

"Very much."

"I might be persuaded." He caught her hand

and led her toward the bed. "If you feed me enough."

While she sat cross-legged beside him, feeding him sips of wine and bites of sandwich, Drew leaned back against the pillows, content to watch her. She was a source of constant delight. Especially when she was able to put the pressure of her work behind her.

She stopped eating to study him more closely. "You have a very smug look on your face, Mr. Hampton. What are you thinking?"

"That I haven't felt this relaxed in such a long time."

"Yeah." She offered him the last bite of sandwich, then reached for the Twinkie.

As she unwrapped it and held it to his mouth, he grinned. "You're seriously bribing me, aren't you, Ms. Sullivan?"

"Absolutely. I have my reasons, of course."

"Of course." He reached for the sash of her robe and untied it while she offered him another bite, and then another, until it was gone.

"And now I suppose I'll have to live up to my half of the bargain." He gave her a sly smile.

"Right again."

He kept his eyes steady on hers as he slid the robe from her shoulders. As his hands began moving over her, she felt the quick rush of heat, and the slow curling sensation deep inside. Her hand trembled, threatening to spill the wine.

"Drew. Quick. Either drink this or take it away."

He merely smiled. "It's your problem, Lessie. I'm just living up to our agreement."

She lifted it to her lips and drained the glass.

"You're in a hurry for that kissing thing, aren't you?" He began drawing her closer.

"You bet." She let the empty glass fall to the floor as he began running wet nibbling kisses up her arm, across her shoulder, along the smooth column of her throat.

Suddenly she gasped as he shifted and rolled, pinning her beneath him. And then, as warm night breezes drifted through the open balcony, they were swept once more into that deep dark pool of desire.

Chapter 12

Celeste awoke and lay very still, trying to get her bearings.

Get her bearings.

An apt phrase, she thought. She'd been lost ever since Drew walked back into her life. Completely lost, and floundering. And hoping that no one noticed her state of confusion. It was so unlike her to be muddled about anything. She'd always been so clear. So straight-thinking. But when it came to Drew, all her common sense fled.

She lay on her side, watching him as he slept. How she'd missed him. That quick, dangerous smile that always did strange things to her heart. Those gray eyes, at once smiling and mysterious.

And that trim, muscled body that brought such pleasure to hers. But it was so much more than physical. She'd missed the way he always seemed to know exactly when she'd reached her limit, whether it was patience or energy or good humor. He'd see her starting to fade and would take over without any seeming effort. Like the way he fed her when she forgot to eat. Or soothed her when her temper flared. Or persuaded her to take a break when he could see her energy begin to flag.

That was the most wonderful thing about Drew. Whenever she was with him, she felt pampered. Cherished. As though she were the most important person in his life.

He was, she realized, her best friend. Her very best friend. And she'd missed him so much.

It occurred to her that she hadn't awakened feeling this content in a very long time. She felt thoroughly rested and thoroughly loved.

She touched a finger to the dark hair that had fallen over his forehead. How she loved looking at him asleep. All that restless energy spent. All that keen edge of danger oddly at peace.

He lay facing her, his leg tossed possessively over hers, one arm flung around her waist. She was reminded of the words he'd whispered to her just before drifting off to sleep.

I'm holding on to you for dear life, Lessie. I'm never going to let you get away again.

But she hadn't been the one who'd walked away. It had been Drew's choice to go. That knowledge still had the power to sting. And now he was back. Acting as though whatever had happened between them was now forgotten. As though the past year was simply wiped away with a single kiss. And in the blink of an eye they'd fallen back into their old routine.

Foolish, she knew. But she had no one to blame but herself. This had been her choice.

No promises, he'd said. And she had agreed to that, as well. Maybe because it suited her. She had known early in life that she wanted the same nomadic existence as her parents and grandparents. She wanted, needed, to be free to move on when the current job was done to her satisfaction.

But what did Drew want? There had been a time when she'd thought she knew him as well as she knew herself. Knew his thoughts and dreams and hopes for the future. But that had been before. Before he'd shattered her world, and her heart, by walking away. Now, though he seemed to be the same sweet, considerate man she'd known and loved, he was also a stranger. There were secrets inside him that he no longer shared with her. Places he could go, where she couldn't follow.

''Hmmm. Looks awfully serious.''

At his voice she looked down to see him watching her, though he hadn't made a sound.

He reached a hand to her cheek. "Regrets?"

She shook her head. "No. How about you?"

"How could I regret what we shared all night?" He dragged her close and brushed soft kisses over her face. "My only regret is that the night didn't last long enough."

"Not long enough?" That brought laughter to her eyes. "Do you realize we just spent the entire night loving?"

"Yeah." He grinned. "Like two greedy kids locked in a candy store."

It was true, she realized. They'd indulged their every fantasy, barely taking the time to doze before rousing themselves to enjoy more.

At times their lovemaking had been as easy, as hesitant as two innocents. At other times they'd been surprised by the explosion of passion that would erupt like a volcano, whirling them down into a dark pool of desire.

Celeste sighed as he began nibbling at her neck. "We ought to think about getting dressed."

"Yeah. In a minute." He pressed his mouth to a trail of freckles that paraded across her shoulder.

With each movement of his lips, she could feel the heat growing, the need increasing. "Drew. We should be getting up."

"You're right. But I have to see where these freckles end." He paused at the swell of her breast. "Look at that. Another one here." He touched his lips to the spot and heard her little sigh of pleasure. "And here..."

Thoughts of getting dressed were forgotten.

In fact, all thought fled as she brought her arms around his waist and held on while he took her on a slow, delicious ride straight to paradise.

"It can't be after noon." Celeste caught sight of the clock and sat straight up in bed.

Drew lay beside her, his arms and legs tangled with hers, the sheets twisted beneath him. He reached for her and drew her down beside him, cradling her in the curve of his arm. "Relax, Lessie. It isn't the end of the world if you're late for work."

"Late for..." She put a hand on his chest and struggled to sit up. "Daniel has probably been phoning my suite since early this morning, and wondering where in the world I am."

Drew pointed to the bedside phone. "Feel free to call him."

"From here?" She shook her head. "I'd rather not have the entire staff speculating on why I was calling from your room."

"Suit yourself." Drew pressed his lips to a tangle of hair at her temple. "How about if I call and order some room service?"

The mention of food made her realize she was starving. "Do we have time?"

"Like I said. You're the boss. What do you think?"

She nodded. "I'd like that. I'm really hungry."

He sat up and picked up the receiver. "What do you feel like? Breakfast or lunch?"

She shrugged. "Whatever you're having."

As he gave his order Celeste started to shimmy out of bed. He snagged her around the waist and pulled her down on his lap while he continued talking. Then, hanging up the phone, he framed her face with his hands and drew her head down for a long, drugging kiss.

Against her lips he murmured, "Trina in Room Service said it would take at least half an hour."

"Good." She brushed her mouth over his cheek, loving the rough, scratchy feel of his beard against her lips. "That'll give us time to shower."

He arched a brow. "I think we could put the time to better use than that."

Celeste burst into gales of laughter. "You can't be serious. Now I know you're a glutton."

"Uh-hmm." He kissed her again, drawing it out until she felt her head begin to spin.

The rush of heat caught her by surprise. Where did this need come from? How could she possibly want more?

Ignoring the question, she wrapped herself around him, letting him take her wherever he chose.

"I can't get enough of you, Lessie." His eyes grew hot and fierce as he tangled his hands in her hair and pulled her head back, savaging her throat. "I'll never have enough of you."

"It's the same for me, Drew. What have you done to me? I can't believe what's happening to both of us."

She'd thought, after such a night, loving until they were sated, that there would be no new places to explore.

Drew proved her wrong again.

A short time later, they looked up at a knock on the door.

Celeste froze. "That can't be room service already."

Drew glanced at the clock. "A half hour exactly." He chuckled against her throat. "You run a very disciplined hotel, Ms. Sullivan."

"You'd think, just this once, they could be a little late."

That had him roaring with laughter as he called, "Just a minute. I'll be right there."

As he struggled into his jeans, Celeste scrambled out of bed and dashed past him, locking herself in the bathroom.

Drew walked to the parlor door to let the waiter in. "'Morning, Billy."

"Good afternoon, Mr. Hampton." The young

man stepped carefully over Celeste's sandals, still lying by the door, and nodded toward the balcony table. "Would you like me to serve lunch out there?"

"No thanks, Billy. Just leave everything on that serving cart." Drew signed the tab and reached into his pocket for the tip.

"Thank you, sir. You have a nice day now."

"You too, Billy."

He saw the young man's gaze skim over the yellow shorts and top lying carelessly beside a chair before letting himself out.

Drew was still debating whether or not to tell Celeste when she came out of the bedroom wearing his hotel robe.

"Oh." She breathed deeply. "I smell coffee."

"Yeah. And food." Drew motioned toward the balcony. "Want to eat first, or shower?"

"Eat," she said at once. "Then I'll have the strength to shower."

They carried the covered trays to the table, and filled two cups with hot, steaming coffee.

While she sipped, Celeste uncovered the first plate. "Now let's see what you ordered." Her eyes widened. "Oh, Drew. A cheese omelette." She uncovered a second plate to reveal French toast.

"I thought we could share."

"We might." She glanced at the covered plates in front of him. "What are you hiding over there?"

He uncovered a sizzling platter of steak, and a second plate containing a variety of toast and breakfast pastries.

"Think this is enough to replenish all the calories we've been burning?"

She laughed as she slid a portion of the omelette onto a plate and passed the rest to him. "It's a good start. But will it hold us until dinnertime?"

He was smiling as he glanced at her. "I think, Ms. Sullivan, that will depend upon what we do between now and this evening."

She was shaking her head as she dug into her food. "Not a chance, Prince Charming. I have an inn to run."

He merely grinned as he helped himself to the rest of the omelette and half the steak. "Just in case I can change your mind about that, I'm planning to fortify myself."

They were still arguing the fact an hour later when Celeste pushed away from the table and started toward the bathroom. After only a couple of steps through the parlor she paused and caught sight of her discarded clothing.

"Oh, no." She clapped a hand to her mouth.

"What's wrong?" Drew came up beside her.

"My things. Why didn't I just print up a big sign that reads Celeste Spent The Night With Drew Hampton? You realize, don't you, that Billy is already downstairs telling everybody what he saw in your room?''

''What he saw was a pile of clothing. I doubt he's ever seen you in anything but your business suits, so there's no reason for him to think they're yours. Besides, do you really think Billy cares who I spent the night with?''

''I suppose not. But I do, Mr. Hampton.''

Drew was still laughing as she grabbed up her clothes and shoes and headed toward the bathroom.

As she stripped and stepped into the shower, she heard a sound and found Drew standing behind her.

''Drew.'' Laughing, she backed up, until she found herself under the warm spray.

''I was lonely out there.'' He picked up the soap and joined her. ''Besides, I figured you'd need somebody to wash your back.''

''How considerate of you. It seems to me you were always very good at that.''

His smile was quick. ''I'm the best.''

''So you say.'' She turned away and said over her shoulder. ''Go ahead and prove it.''

He ran the soap in slow, sensuous circles over her back, across her shoulders, down her arms and heard her little sigh of pleasure.

He leaned close and handed her the soap. ''All right. You've had enough. Now it's my turn.''

She was laughing as he stood under the spray

and wriggled like a puppy while she ran the soap over his chest, his arms, the flat planes of his stomach.

Suddenly he took the soap from her hands and tossed it aside.

"Drew, what are you doing?"

With a dangerous smile he bent his head and took one slick, wet nipple into his mouth. Madness gripped them both. Wave after wave of pleasure shot through them as he lifted her, wrapped her legs around him, and pressed her against the wall of the shower. She moved with him, climbed with him, while the warm water continued to cascade over them.

"What do you think?" Drew sat on the sofa with his arm around Celeste, who was wearing his hotel robe, her hair wrapped in a towel. "Do we go downstairs for what's left of the day? Or do we stay up here and order in?"

Celeste laid her head on his shoulder, too content to do more than smile. "What you're really asking is, do I want to face the staff today, or put it off until the morning?"

"Yeah." He grinned. "There's that. But there's also the fact that it takes a lot of energy to get dressed. So if we stay up here, we can expend that energy on...other things."

"You must be kidding." She turned her head enough to see his face.

He kissed her full on the mouth. "You wouldn't want me to answer that, Lessie."

"Okay." She sighed, and lowered her head to his shoulder once more. "I really don't have the energy to dress and face the staff now. So I vote to stay here the rest of the day and evening."

"My kind of woman." He tipped up her face and kissed her again.

"I just don't know how I'll face Billy with another room service delivery."

He squeezed her hand. "You can hide in the bathroom again."

"It won't matter. By this time I'm sure everyone has figured out what's going on."

He nodded. "All right. We'll resort to plan B."

"Which is?"

He thought a minute. "How do you feel about pizza tonight?"

"I'd love it. But I'm not sure it's on the room service menu."

"Even better. I'll look up pizza deliveries in the phone book and have one brought over."

She brightened. "Very clever, Mr. Hampton. We don't have to face Billy."

"And we can have pizza in bed."

"In bed?"

He gave her a devilish smile. "Trust me. It's the best way to enjoy it."

Chapter 13

"Good morning, Ms. Sullivan." Drew stepped from his room and caught Celeste's hand as she stepped from her suite across the hall.

After showering together, they'd parted minutes earlier, when she'd wrapped herself in his robe and darted back to her own place to dress for the day.

She was wearing a cream-colored suit with a long jacket over a very short skirt. She looked, Drew thought, like an ad for businesswoman of the year. A look, he realized, that always managed to turn him on.

Drew linked his fingers with hers and paused at the elevator. "You look wonderful, Lessie."

"I feel wonderful. I can't remember when I've

spent such a lazy day as we had yesterday. Thank you, Drew. It was such a special gift.''

He lifted her hand to his mouth. ''My pleasure, ma'am. It was special for me, too. Any time you want to take another day off, just let me know. I'm always happy to oblige.''

They stepped into the elevator and watched as the doors glided shut.

Seeing the way she held herself stiffly as the numbers flashed by, Drew touched a hand to her cheek. ''You're not still worried about facing the staff, are you?''

She shrugged, looking uncomfortable. ''It's going to be awkward. But it has to be done.''

''It's going to be fine. You'll see. You have a great staff. And if there are any rumors, it's only because they genuinely care about you. But you're a woman, and free to live your life as you choose.''

''I know. But we're all like family.''

''Which is why they love you.''

When they reached the lobby the elevator doors parted and Drew stepped back, allowing her to precede him.

The first person they spotted was Jeremiah, looking distinguished in a gray, double-breasted suit, with a red carnation at his lapel.

''Good morning, Miss Celeste. Mr. Hampton. My, don't you two look rested.'' He gave them a wide, welcoming smile before turning to Celeste.

"You were missed yesterday, but I'm sure I speak for all of us when I say that I'm so glad you finally took a well-deserved day off." Seeing the slight flush on her cheeks he added diplomatically, "Looks like it's going to be another perfect summer day."

"Yes." Celeste cleared her throat. "Are there any big luncheons planned for the courtyard or ballroom today, Jeremiah?"

"The Billings Corporation will be occupying the courtyard, starting at eleven. The town council will be holding their monthly meeting in the library at noon. As always, they're hoping you'll stop by and say a few words of greeting. And I believe the ballroom will be used by the state high school forensics finalists. You might want to check with young O'Malley on the time scheduled for that one."

"Thank you, Jeremiah. I'll do that."

As she started away the old man called, "I spoke with your grandfather."

She paused. "Is he here?"

"Not yet." Jeremiah glanced from Celeste to Drew. "He said his flight was delayed. But not to worry. He'll be here just as soon as he can."

"Thank you, Jeremiah. When did you speak with him?"

"He phoned me last night."

She wrinkled her brow. "I wonder why he didn't call me?"

The old man made a show of removing a piece of lint from his sleeve. "I suppose he didn't want to bother you."

She turned and started toward her office, with Drew beside her. As they passed the front desk Bitsy Hillerman cradled a phone to her shoulder and lifted a hand in greeting.

"Glad to see you, Ms. Sullivan."

"Thank you, Bitsy." As Celeste breezed past, she turned and found Bitsy staring after them while carrying on an animated conversation with the unseen party on the other end of the line.

Minutes later they entered Celeste's office. Her assistant, Daniel, hung up the phone and got to his feet, holding out a pile of paperwork. "Good morning, Ms. Sullivan. Glad to see you back. Here are your phone messages and mail." He turned to Drew. "Good morning, Mr. Hampton."

Drew nodded and offered a greeting.

Celeste took in a breath before asking, "Did I miss anything of importance yesterday?"

Her assistant shook his head and stared at a spot on his desk. "It was a slow day. Nothing to bother you about. We were able to handle everything in your absence. There are, however, several luncheons planned today."

"Jeremiah already filled me in on them." She

glanced at the papers in her hand. "I suppose one of these is my daily calendar?"

"And the weekly schedule as well, Ms. Sullivan, since you weren't here yesterday to go over it with me."

"Thank you, Daniel." She turned away and walked to her inner office, trailed by Drew.

When he closed the door and sat across from her desk, he saw her little frown. "What's wrong?"

"Nothing. Not a thing." She tapped a finger on the pile of papers. "Except that everyone's being so damnably polite, I can hardly stand it."

His smile was quick and easy. "I think you're making too much of this. Nobody was whispering or pointing. They all seemed genuinely happy to see you finally take some time away from your work." He leaned back. "And look at it this way. You still have plenty of time to catch up before your grandfather gets here."

She nodded. "I wonder what's keeping him? He's had more than enough time to fly in from Venice."

Drew had been thinking the same thing. "Unless he was planning on coming by way of Mars." He glanced at the paperwork stacked on her desk. "I think I'll give you some time to deal with that." He stood. "Maybe I'll help myself to a cup of the Old Liberty Tavern's excellent coffee." He paused. "If you give me a quick kiss, I might be persuaded to bring some back for you."

She looked up with a laugh. "I can see that you've picked up some very bad habits in the past day few days, Mr. Hampton." She stood and leaned across the desk.

When he held back she arched a brow. "What's wrong?"

"I'm not the only one with bad habits. Now I suppose you'll want a kiss along with your coffee every morning." Instead of meeting her across the desk he strode around it and dragged her close, kissing her long and slow and deep.

She felt the familiar rush of heat, and the way her head began to slowly empty of all thought. She sighed. "You could just skip the coffee, as long as you promise to kiss me like that every morning. I think it packs a bigger jolt than caffeine."

"You've got yourself a deal, Ms. Sullivan." He strolled out of her office and made his way to the coffee shop.

For Celeste the day went by in a blur of work. It seemed to take her twice as long to handle her paperwork and respond to the phone messages that had piled up in her absence.

Then there were the demands of three separate luncheons, all expecting a personal appearance by the hotel manager. By late afternoon she was grateful for the extra rest she'd managed to store up the previous day. She was more aware than ever of the grueling schedule she'd been keeping in the past year. How had she managed without collapsing? It occurred to her that she had probably been running on pure adrenalin.

She looked up when Drew paused beside her, holding out a cup. "What's this?"

"Herbal tea. It'll give you a lift until you have time to stop for dinner." He glanced at his watch. "Which I'd suggest very soon now, unless you'd like to drop from sheer exhaustion."

"I'll wait until Grandpa Sully gets here. I'm sure he'll want me to join him for dinner."

"Lessie, it's way past dinnertime."

He saw the look on her face and quickly touched a hand to her shoulder to steady her. "Now don't go thinking something's wrong. I'm sure he's just held up by business. You know what kind of days you put in. His are probably no easier."

"But he has able assistants, Drew. And he said he was coming." She couldn't hide her concern.

Seeing the head of catering striding her way, wearing a look of distress, Drew closed a hand over hers and squeezed gently. "You deal with this latest crisis. I'll find Jeremiah and see if he's heard anything about your grandfather."

She gave him a grateful smile. "Thanks, Drew."

He leaned close to whisper, "You can thank me later."

Then he was gone.

The day had long ago bled into evening, and evening into night, when Drew found Celeste shaking hands with a delegation of nurses who had come to town to check out the Old Liberty Tavern's accommodations for a proposed convention the following year.

He waited until they were gone, then walked up behind her and began massaging the taut muscles of her shoulders.

"Oh, that feels so good." She allowed herself to lean into him a moment, loving the feel of his strong hands on her. Then she turned her head to glance at him. "What did you learn about Grandpa Sully?"

"It seems he's delayed his flight for another day."

She turned to face him, her brows drawn together in a thoughtful frown. "Did he say why?"

Drew shook his head. "No reason given. Jeremiah just said he'd heard from him, and he expects to be in tomorrow."

She gave a sigh of resignation, pressing her forehead to his. "I'm sure he has his reasons."

She stepped back abruptly when she saw one of the bellmen approaching.

Drew saw the weariness in her eyes. "Time to call it a day, Ms. Sullivan. I intend to order up dinner."

She managed a smile. "My place or yours?"

"Yours. But it won't be up there for a while. I thought that would give you time to go upstairs and take a long, soaking bath."

"What makes you think I want a bath?"

He gave her one of those quick, heart-stopping grins. "You know you like nothing better than to soak in the tub after a long day. And if you go right now, you can have the place to yourself. If you delay another half an hour, you'll have company, whether you like it or not."

"And who might my company be?"

"A frog. Who happens to like splashing in your bath. Now, do you want to tell me what you'd like for dinner?"

"Frog legs." She couldn't help laughing at his menacing look. "Well, I guess that means I'd better change my mind." She thought a minute, then shrugged. "My brain's too fogged. You'll have to order for me."

He touched a finger to her lips. Just a touch, but she felt the heat as surely as a kiss. "I like ordering for you. In fact, I can't think of anything I like better than just taking care of you."

He watched as she headed toward the elevator.

Then he turned in the opposite direction, planning their menu.

"This is nice." Celeste had tied her hair up with combs while soaking in the bath. Now damp little tendrils had pulled loose in the night air to kiss her cheeks. "I think I'm almost glad Grandpa Sully is delayed."

She had slipped into a pale green silk kimono. From the way it skimmed her body, revealing every line and curve, it was obvious that she wore nothing under it. A fact that had Drew's heart beating a little faster than normal as he poured cool, pale champagne into two tulip glasses.

He'd changed from his business suit to faded denims and a silk T-shirt the color of putty.

He walked to the balcony railing and handed her the glass before touching the rim of his against it. "Then, here's to your grandfather, and to his many delays. May he continue the pattern for many days to come."

They both smiled and sipped.

She glanced at the covered trays on the serving trolley. "What did you order for dinner?"

"If I tell you, it won't be a surprise. And you did tell me to order for you."

She pouted. "I don't know what I was thinking. You know I hate surprises."

He merely smiled. "That's not true. You just

hate not being in control of everything. But everybody likes to be surprised now and then.''

"I don't.''

He leaned a hip against the railing to study her. "You didn't like my surprise visit?''

"Not at first.''

"Uh-huh. And now?''

"Now I'm getting used to the idea.''

"So am I.'' He skimmed a fingertip up her arm and felt the way she shivered. His grin was quick and dangerous. "I'm getting used to a lot of ideas.''

"Such as?''

He nodded toward the food. "Those covered trays will keep everything hot for hours.''

"The point being...?'' She couldn't hide the laughter that warmed her words, since she had anticipated where this was leading.

He touched a finger to the deep vee of her kimono, loving the way her eyes suddenly darkened. "It wouldn't hurt to put off eating for a while and...indulge in other pleasures.''

"You don't think we ought to eat first? Just so we have the necessary strength to...indulge those other pleasures?''

He set aside his glass, then took hers from her hand and set it beside his. Keeping his eyes steady on hers he untied the sash of her gown and began sliding it from her shoulders. His gaze skimmed

her, and she saw the heat shimmer in those gray
depths in the moment before he drew her close and
covered her mouth with his.

The kiss had been worth waiting all day for. It
was all heat and flash and fire. And wild, desperate
need. A need so unexpected, a hunger so deep, it
caught them both by surprise.

"Did you say that food would keep for hours?"

He laughed. Then groaned. And lost himself
once more in her.

Chapter 14

Drew lay in Celeste's big bed, one arm under his head, the other cradling her as she slept in his arms. He felt like singing Patrick Sullivan's praises to the heavens. Because of his unexpected delay, they'd been given one more night together. It had seemed like a special gift. One they had enjoyed like eager children. They'd teased each other shamelessly. Laughed over silly, private jokes. And made love with a fever born of desperation.

Their marvelous meal of lemon chicken and pasta had added to the festive feelings. They'd fed each other, sipped champagne, and much later had shared coffee and luscious chocolate-dipped strawberries.

When they'd finally come to bed they left the draperies open so they could see the night sky. They'd even had the good fortune of spotting a shooting star, and Celeste had squeezed her eyes tightly shut while making a wish. Drew had made a wish of his own. And though they both claimed to scoff at superstition, neither had been willing to reveal their wish to the other.

He loved watching her. Loved the way she slept, deep and dreamless, like a child. Golden shafts of moonlight played over her face, gilding her skin, turning her hair to fire. It occurred to him that he would be perfectly content to spend the rest of his life watching her like this.

The rest of his life.

Dangerous thoughts. He frowned, as he considered all the complications. They were both driven to be the best at their chosen careers. Careers that would never permit them to be in the same place for more than a few months, or on the rare occasion, a year at the most.

How could even the most devoted lovers keep a long-distance relationship alive under such circumstances?

Celeste sighed in her sleep and rolled toward him, her hair spilling over his arm, her hand resting on his heart. He pressed his mouth to her temple and breathed her in.

It wasn't fair, he thought with a sudden rush of temper. He'd put in the longest year of his life, trying to get her out of his mind. He'd taken jobs no one else would even consider, just to keep himself from thinking about what he'd given up. And now, after the most bizarre set of circumstances, he was right back where he'd started. Only this time it was so much more intense. Maybe because they were both older now. And, he hoped, wiser. Certainly wise enough to know how much suffering they would endure when they were forced to part this time.

This time.

Now that he'd tasted her again, how could he bear to leave her? He didn't think he had the strength to go through it all again. Still, what was the alternative? Commuting across continents to snatch an occasional night together? That hardly qualified as a relationship.

Would she suffer as well? Or would she simply bury herself in work and put him out of her mind? This time, if she did, it would be forever. She'd already told him she couldn't bear to go through it all again.

He found it impossible to sleep. As night drifted toward dawn, he lay awake, tormenting himself with thoughts of what was. And thoughts of what might have been. If only they'd chosen different paths.

* * *

Celeste awoke suddenly, aware that she was alone in her bed. She didn't know why that should alarm her. She'd grown accustomed to waking alone. And yet, in just these brief days and nights since Drew had walked back into her life, everything had changed. She'd allowed herself to care about him again. To feel things that might be better left alone.

And she'd learned to love waking with him in her arms.

She considered herself a smart, sophisticated woman. And yet she'd walked into this with her eyes wide open, knowing that Drew had the ability to hurt her like no one else ever could.

She'd thought herself over him. And yet, with one touch, one smile, she'd tumbled back into his arms, and into his bed.

No regrets, she warned herself. When he left, as he surely would, she wouldn't allow herself to play that game of regrets again. The first time around she'd questioned everything she'd ever said and done. Would he have stayed if only she'd been more involved in his life, and less in her career? Had he needed more of her than she'd been willing to give? Was she a selfish, self-centered person for wanting to succeed at the family business? But gradually she'd come to realize that love, true love, finds a way through even the most difficult and demanding circumstances. She had to face the fact that they hadn't loved each other enough to make it work. Or else, they were simply too young and inexperienced to find their way through the maze of roadblocks that had stood in their path.

In the soft light of morning she saw Drew standing on the balcony, staring off into the distance. Her heart did a little flip at the sight of him, so handsome and rugged. She studied the firm line of his jaw in profile. She couldn't decide if he was sad or angry.

He'd apparently dressed quickly, leaving his jeans unsnapped, riding low on his waist. Barefoot and shirtless, he leaned his hands against the rail and stood as still as a statue.

Where had he gone in his mind? Wherever it was, it wasn't a particularly happy place. He appeared to be in a thoughtful, pensive mood.

He turned and caught sight of her watching him. As he started toward her, his smile returned, quick and charming.

"Good morning, sleepyhead."

"'Morning." She sat up and shoved her hair from her eyes.

He sank down on the edge of the mattress and closed his hands over her shoulders, drawing her close as he brushed his lips over hers.

She felt the familiar jolt to her system and mar-

veled that such a simple thing as a morning kiss
could pack such a punch.

"What's wrong?" He held her a little away and
stared into her eyes. Was there sadness there? Was
she troubled? Or was he letting his imagination run
wild?

"Nothing. It's just..." She shook her head as if
to clear it. "How long have you been awake?"

"Not long. I was trying to be quiet so I wouldn't
disturb you." He brushed a wayward strand of hair
from her cheek. "You looked so peaceful."

"And you looked as if you were a million miles
away."

He drew her close and pressed soft, whispering
kisses over her forehead. "I was right here, Lessie.
With you."

She could feel her heartbeat begin to race. Could
feel her blood starting to heat and surge through
her veins, in anticipation of what was to come.

"Hold me, Drew. Make love with me one more
time."

"I thought you'd never ask," he whispered as
he took her mouth with his.

Make love. As his hands and lips began to
weave their magic, she thought about the feelings
he'd stirred in her. There was passion, of course.
And heart-stopping desire. But there was so much
more. She'd thought, hoped, that it was mere lust
that had taken hold of her heart, and held it still.

But she now knew, without a doubt, that what she felt for him went much deeper.

It was love. Total, absolute love. Sweet heaven. As she gave herself up to him, she felt her heart trip, then stumble. She'd gone and lost her heart to the one man who could break it beyond repair.

She held on as he took her on a fast, dizzying spin. She felt herself soaring, then burning as brightly as the morning sun, before drifting gently back to earth.

The tears that burned in the back of her throat were swallowed quietly. It wouldn't do to let him know her secret, when he would probably be gone before the day was over.

"Do you have time to join me for breakfast?" Drew was holding her hand in his, their fingers linked, as they stepped into the elevator and watched the numbers flash by.

He seemed subdued. Though he'd smiled and joked while they'd showered and dressed, Celeste had sensed his air of distraction. It had her more uneasy than she cared to admit.

Was he already mentally distancing himself from her? Was he searching his mind for the best way to say his goodbyes, so that he could move on without an ugly scene?

"I should really get to my office and see if Daniel has heard from Grandpa Sully."

He nodded, still watching the flashing numbers above the door. As if, she thought, he didn't want to look her in the eye. Finally he turned to her. "Maybe I'll go along with you. I can always grab some coffee later."

Just as the doors glided open, he released her hand and they stepped apart before exiting the elevator.

Celeste glanced around, expecting to see Jeremiah in the lobby. As she passed the front desk she called out, "Good morning, Bitsy."

"Good morning, Ms. Sullivan. Mr. Hampton."

"Have you seen Jeremiah this morning?"

The girl shook her head. "Sorry, Ms. Sullivan. I haven't seen him since I came on duty an hour ago."

"That's strange." She started toward her office, with Drew beside her. "I can't recall the last time Jeremiah wasn't here ahead of me, standing guard in the foyer."

When she stepped into her office Daniel O'Malley got to his feet and held out a handful of papers. "Good morning, Ms. Sullivan. Mr. Hampton."

She accepted the papers from his hand. "Do you happen to know where Jeremiah is?"

The young man nodded. "He went with the driver to the airport to pick up your grandfather."

"What time was that?"

The young man glanced at his watch. "I'd say

at least two hours ago. They should be here any time now."

"You'll let me know when they get here?"

"I will, Ms. Sullivan."

She took a deep breath and started toward her inner office, with Drew trailing behind. Once inside he closed the door and watched as she dropped her mail and phone messages on the desk without even glancing at them. Instead she strode to the window and crossed her arms over her chest.

What was the matter with her? She hadn't seen Grandpa Sully in ages. Not since her sister Lizbeth's wedding. Usually when they got together, it was a joyous reunion, with both of them talking a mile a minute while they exchanged news about the latest acquisitions by Sullivan Hotels, or the latest sales.

A week ago she'd have been bursting with pride about her success here at the tavern. She would have enumerated the wedding parties, wine tastings, banquets, art exhibits, all of which enhanced the earning power of this place. And if her grandfather had suggested that it was time to put the Old Liberty Tavern up for sale while it was a hot commodity, she'd have felt nothing but a sense of pride. After all, it was her hard work and business savvy that had earned another profit for the family business.

Something had happened between now and last

week. Something that had taken the edge off winning. Whatever it was, it frightened her. And she didn't know quite how to fight it. She felt a trickle of fear along her spine.

When Drew cleared his throat, her head came up sharply. She'd been so deep in thought, she'd forgotten that she wasn't alone. Had forgotten that he was here, watching, and probably sensing her nerves.

"I think I'll get that coffee now. Want some?"

"Thanks. That'd be…fine, Drew."

She continued to stare out the window as the door behind her softly opened, then closed. She heard Drew exchanging words with Daniel, before silence settled over the office once more.

Suddenly she turned away and pressed her hands to her eyes.

Damn that brilliant sunshine. It was the only reason she could think of for the moisture that suddenly burned.

By the time Drew returned to her office with a tray, Celeste had carefully composed herself. She actually managed to laugh when he uncovered the tray to reveal not only a carafe of coffee, but a freshly baked croissant and a little pot of black cherry jam as well.

"Something to tide you over." He was studying her carefully. A little too carefully, she realized.

She pretended to look at the food, avoiding his eyes. "Nothing for you?"

"I had some coffee while I was waiting."

"Then we'll share."

"Can't. Sorry." He shook his head and took a step back.

Just then there was a knock on her door and Daniel poked his head inside. "Ms. Sullivan, your grandfather just phoned and asked if you and Mr. Hampton would meet him for lunch in the library at noon."

"Noon?" Celeste glanced at her watch. "That's nearly three hours from now. Did he say where he was?"

The young man shook his head. "I'm afraid he didn't. But I believe he was calling from the car. Maybe he and Jeremiah had some stops to make."

She sighed in resignation. "All right. I guess I'll just have to wait until noon to see what he's decided."

When Daniel O'Malley left, Drew saw the worried frown that marred her forehead. He turned toward the door. "I'll see you at noon. If I'm late, just go ahead without me, and I'll meet you and your grandfather in the library."

"How could you be late? Where are you going, Drew?"

"To my room." He pulled open the door. "I have some work to take care of."

Celeste stared at the closed door, then slumped down at her desk, pushing aside the coffee and croissant. The thought of eating anything, or even sipping strong hot coffee, had suddenly lost its appeal.

Everyone, it seemed, had work to do or errands to run. Everyone but her. Even the thought of all those phone messages to return and documents to read and sign, held no interest.

She wanted this over with. Wanted her life back the way it was before.

She pressed her hands to her eyes. That wasn't so. If she were going to be honest with herself, she'd have to admit that in truth, she wanted what she had now, with what she'd had before. Her life here at the Old Liberty Tavern, but with Drew in it.

There. She'd allowed herself to admit the one thing she knew she couldn't have. And she had nobody to blame but herself for this mess.

Her idyllic little balloon was about to crash and burn at noon.

Chapter 15

"Celeste, my darlin' little lass." Paddy Sullivan hurried across the room to embrace his granddaughter. Then he held her a little away and gave her a long, steady look. "Oh, you're looking grand. So fine and rested and fresh."

"So are you, Grandpa Sully." She kissed his cheek. "I swear you never get any older. How is that possible?"

"I'd like to say clean living." He chuckled. "But it's probably because I believe in living life to the fullest. You never know when your number's up, so make every minute count. That's my motto."

He kept his arm around her shoulders as he drew

her toward a round table drawn up in one of the big bay windows of the library. Standing beside it was Jeremiah, dressed in a navy blazer and gray slacks, his face wreathed in smiles.

"Ah, this is perfect," Paddy Sullivan said with a sigh. "My beautiful granddaughter and my oldest friend in the world. It doesn't get any better than this."

Jeremiah winked at Celeste. "Especially when your young, lovely, talented and hardworking granddaughter can boast of such a successful turnaround for a once-failing inn."

"There's that, to be sure." Paddy poured a tall glass of bottled water and offered it to Celeste, then poured another for himself.

He lifted the glass to his lips and drank deeply.

He looked up when Drew paused in the doorway. "Ah, Andrew. I was just about to ask where you were."

Drew studied Celeste, noting her hands, holding stiffly to the glass to hide her nerves. There might have been a time when he wouldn't have recognized the pose. Now he knew her so well. Knew just how much she was struggling to hold herself together.

He turned to her grandfather. "Sorry. I had some business to see to before our luncheon."

Paddy Sullivan nodded. "Getting all your ducks in a row I suppose, before we make our deal." He set down his glass. "I was just about to tell my granddaughter how proud I am of the work she's done here at the tavern. It's gone from one of the worst Sullivan Hotels to one of the most profitable. No small accomplishment, as I'm sure you can appreciate."

Drew caught the look in Celeste's eyes at her grandfather's words. Pleasure mingled with pain in those green depths, and he knew something of the complicated feelings she was being forced to endure. Even while she was being praised, she was mentally preparing herself for what was to come. She was about to be removed from the source of so much pride. Not an easy thing under the best of circumstances. But this time, it was made twice as difficult because of the personal and complicated nature of the deal.

They looked up as a waiter wheeled in a serving cart and began removing covered trays and placing them on the table.

The young waiter turned to Paddy Sullivan. "Would you like the covers removed, sir?"

"Not yet, son." Paddy nodded toward a bottle of champagne. "But you might want to open that. I suspect we'll be drinking a toast shortly."

Without a word the waiter uncorked the champagne and filled four tulip glasses before leaving the room.

Paddy handed a glass to his granddaughter, and

another to Drew, before picking up two more and
handing one to Jeremiah and holding his own aloft.

"Here's to my darlin' Celeste, who has once
again worked her magic for the sake of Sullivan
Hotels."

They touched glasses before taking a taste.

After one sip Paddy smiled. "My favorite brand,
darlin' lass. The finest champagne in the world.
You do know how to stock a bar."

"I had a good teacher." To ease the lump in her
throat she forced herself to take another sip.

"True enough. I've always encouraged a well-
stocked bar and the best chef money can buy. They
both go a long way toward making the client comfortable. But the most important thing of all in
every Sullivan hotel is the staff. People who enjoy
people.

"Well." Paddy glanced around at the others.
"Why don't we eat first? I don't know about the
rest of you, but I'm famished." He held Celeste's
chair, then sat to her left, leaving Drew to sit on
her right, with Jeremiah across from her.

As they uncovered their plates, Paddy smiled.
"I hope you don't mind that I ordered for all of
us. It seemed simpler than having to deal with the
constant interruptions of wait staff."

Celeste nodded, wondering how she would manage to eat a bite, despite the fact that the medal-
lions of beef in port-rosemary sauce smelled heav-

enly. Leave it to her grandfather to order the finest foods just before condemning her to a fate worse than death.

Paddy and Jeremiah were in high spirits, sipping champagne, eating with gusto, and exchanging dozens of reminiscences.

"This reminds me of that time in Paris." Paddy paused to take another sip of champagne. "Do you remember, my friend?"

Jeremiah nodded. "We were fresh out of college, and working our way across Europe. We'd pooled our resources and were eating in the finest little café. And seated across the room was the most beautiful creature, with autumn hair and green eyes and..."

"...and a scowling grandmother," Paddy put in with a laugh, "who was ready to skin the brazen young Irishman staring at her granddaughter like a lovesick fool."

Jeremiah picked up the thread of the story, aware that Celeste and Drew were hearing it for the first time. "We put our heads together and decided that instead of a generous tip to the waiter, we'd spend the last of our money on a bottle of the café's best champagne, which we sent to the lovely creature's table."

"Of course," Paddy continued, "the old grandmother had no choice but to invite us to join them, though I'm sure it was against her better judgment.

And by the time we'd finished off the bottle, she'd agreed to allow us to accompany her and her granddaughter home.''

The two old men were laughing at the memory.

Paddy laid a hand over Celeste's. ''Which is how that gorgeous creature happened to become your grandmother, and pass on that lovely red hair and those bewitching green eyes to you, darlin' lass.''

''You picked up Grandma in a French café?'' Celeste couldn't stop the laughter that bubbled in her throat.

''I simply couldn't help myself. I knew, the moment I saw her, that she was the one.''

Jeremiah nodded his agreement. ''I'll never forget Paddy leaning over to whisper, 'See that redhead? She's going to be my wife.' And within five years she was.''

''Five years? Grandpa Sully, I'm surprised at you. What took you so long?'' Celeste asked.

Paddy drained his glass. ''I had to prove myself worthy. Her father was a wealthy banker. And I was just a young man with a dream. But I was willing to do whatever I had to in order to make my dream a reality.'' He set aside his glass. ''You see, darlin', there's something in a man's nature, even the most brash among us, that drives us to prove ourselves to the woman who'll be our mate. I could have stepped into her father's business in a heartbeat, for I had real talent with figures. But I knew that if I were to one day become bank president like her father, I'd always wonder if I rose to the top because of my own talent, or because I was married to the boss's daughter.''

"And so you went off and followed your own dream instead."

"That I did. If I've learned anything in this life, it's that a man has to take a risk sometimes, in order to turn his dreams into reality."

He polished off the last of his meal and sat back with a sigh. He glanced at Drew's plate. "You didn't like the food, Andrew?"

"It was fine. I just don't have much of an appetite."

Paddy watched the way Celeste moved the food around her plate. "I suppose it is a bit rich for a midday meal. But this is, after all, a celebration. Maybe I should have held off until dinnertime." He lifted a silver server and poured himself coffee, then arched a brow. "Anyone else care for some?"

Celeste and Drew refused, while Jeremiah nodded and accepted a steaming cup.

It occurred to Drew that these two old friends were in high good humor. As though they were sharing a private joke.

"Now." Paddy sipped his coffee before looking at Drew. "I'm sure you've had plenty of time to study our little operation here in Liberty."

"More than enough time."

"Grandpa Sully…" Celeste put a hand on his arm, but he merely patted it and ignored her attempt to interrupt, keeping his attention focused on Drew.

"Then I'm sure you'll admit that this place would be the buy of a lifetime, Andrew."

Drew nodded. "It would, indeed. It has an impressive profit-and-loss record."

"So then you've recommended to the board of Van Dorn Hotels that they make an offer to purchase the Old Liberty Tavern?"

"Sir…"

"Grandpa Sully…" This time Celeste was determined to interrupt. She shot a quelling look at Drew, then charged ahead. "I want to know why you're so determined to sell something I've worked so hard to make into a success."

"Why? Because, darlin' lass, that's the nature of our business." He kept his tone patient. "You know that. You've done it so many times now, starting when you were just a wee child following after your parents, you could do it by rote. We Sullivans take over a failing hotel, pour our heart and soul into it, and when it becomes profitable enough, we add it to our stable of winning hotels, or put it on the market to the highest bidder, so we can move on to the next challenge. Why should this one be any different?"

She shrugged, wondering how to explain what she didn't even understand herself. "I don't know. I keep telling myself this place is no different from the others. But it is, and I don't understand why. Maybe in a year or two I'll be ready to move on. But not yet, Grandpa Sully. Not now. I just don't think I'm ready to let go of this yet. I'd like us to keep it around for a while longer."

"Darlin'." He patted her hand. "This isn't personal. It's business." He turned to Drew. "I'll ask you again, Andrew. Have you recommended to the board of Van Dorn Hotels that they buy the Old Liberty Tavern?"

"That would be my recommendation." Drew kept his gaze fixed on his plate, avoiding Celeste's eyes. "If I were in a position to offer advice."

Paddy studied him with cool speculation. "What are you saying, Andrew? I thought that's why you were here."

"I'm here because I was sent here by my company. But I'm no longer with Van Dorn Hotels. I resigned my position, effective this morning. And in so doing, disqualified myself from any part of this deal."

"You quit?" Celeste turned to stare at Drew.

He gave a curt nod of his head.

"But you worked so hard to climb to the top. And you were almost there, Drew."

He refused to look at her. "It doesn't matter."

"It doesn't matter? Drew..."

Paddy interrupted, watching Drew intently. "Where will you go, Andrew?"

"I don't know." Drew shoved back his chair and got to his feet, running a hand through his hair in agitation. "I haven't thought that far ahead. But I realized that I could no longer fairly represent Van Dorn Hotels in this deal. I can no longer remain objective about it."

"And why is that?"

Before he could answer, Celeste was on her feet, hurrying over to touch a hand to his arm. "Oh, Drew. You resigned because of me, didn't you?"

He looked at her, and felt all the misery and uncertainty of the past hours melting away. He was no longer aware of the two old men who sat watching and listening with avid interest. Instead, all he could see was Celeste. Her eyes happy and shining. Her fingers curling into his arm, spreading warmth through his veins.

"I didn't do it just for you, Lessie. I did it for us. We found something here in these short days and nights that we nearly lost forever." His tone lowered. Softened. "There was no way I could walk away from you, from this, again."

"Well." Paddy leaned back, and winked at Jeremiah. "Isn't this an interesting development? Who would have thought?"

The two old men were grinning like conspirators.

"Maybe we ought to leave now." Patrick shoved back his chair and got to his feet, beckoning to Jeremiah. "So you two lovebirds can be alone to…discuss things."

They were almost to the door when Celeste's voice stopped them in their tracks. "Just a minute."

The two old men turned.

"Grandpa Sully, what about the Old Liberty Tavern? Are you still going to negotiate with Van Dorn Hotels?"

He glanced at Jeremiah, and the two men chuckled.

Paddy shrugged. "Let's not talk business now, darlin'. There's time enough for that later, don't you think?"

"No. I need to know right now. After all, it's my future we're discussing."

The old man nodded. "Indeed it is, darlin'. I think it's safe to say that for now, we'll just take this offer off the table. Let Van Dorn Hotels look elsewhere for a winner."

He looked at Drew. "But since you're now available again, the offer I made you a year ago still stands, Andrew."

Drew looked away. "And my answer is still the same, Paddy. My name isn't Sullivan."

His words triggered a memory in Celeste that had her looking from him to her grandfather. "You said that once before." She thought back to that day in the hallway, when she'd first confronted him about leaving. "You said then that you left me because your name wasn't Sullivan."

When he said nothing more she turned to her grandfather. "Was it Drew's decision to leave, Grandpa Sully? Or yours?"

Patrick Sullivan studied his granddaughter, then gave a sigh of resignation. "I suppose I do owe you an explanation, darlin'. Since Andrew is probably too proud a man to ever speak of it himself."

The old man cleared his throat. "Do you remember when I invited Andrew to my lodge in Snug Harbor?"

Celeste nodded.

"I brought him there alone, to discuss his future with the company. And I asked him to accept an executive position. But Andrew thought my offer was too much, too soon."

Celeste turned to Drew. "You...refused an executive position. Despite all your ambitions?"

Before he could answer, Patrick Sullivan interrupted. "He did, lass. In fact, he was afraid that this was all happening because of his relationship with you. I tried to assure him otherwise, but he was having none of it. He told me that he needed to find out for himself if he could really do the job.

And the only way to do that was to leave Sullivan Hotels and see if he had what it takes to succeed in this business without any connections.''

This was all happening too quickly. Celeste couldn't seem to take it all in. For the first time she was beginning to understand why Drew had left so abruptly.

Her eyes narrowed. ''But what about me, Drew? Didn't I matter?''

His voice was rough with emotion. ''More than anything. But I didn't feel I deserved you any more than I deserved the promotion your grandfather was offering me. At the time all I had was a lot of ambition and a few hundred dollars in the bank. Who was I to dare to love one of the heirs to one of the richest, most successful hotel chains in the world?''

''Love? You could claim to love me even while you were planning to leave me?''

His tone was as steely as the look in his eyes. ''I loved you then, and I love you still. But I'll do it on my terms, Lessie, or not at all.''

At his words she felt tears well up in her eyes and was forced to blink hard to hold them at bay. There was no room for tears in a business luncheon. Especially with her grandfather and Jeremiah watching. ''And all this time I thought when you left that you'd used me to get ahead in the business, and then dumped me when a better offer came along with Van Dorn Hotels.''

Paddy's voice was contrite. ''I should have told you the truth, darlin', but I was ashamed of the way I'd botched things. I should have given both of you more time. You were young, and caught in the first throes of love.''

He turned to Drew. ''That offer I made at my lodge still stands. I need to cut back my workload and find time for other things. So does my son. We've earned the right to pass the baton to the next generation. I've always known that both you and Celeste were up to the job. And now that you've resigned your position with Van Dorn, I can't see any reason why you shouldn't return to Sullivan Hotels.'' His brogue thickened. ''I hope I'm not speaking out of turn when I say that I'm thinking you're the perfect partner, not only for my granddaughter, but for us.''

For the space of several minutes Drew couldn't seem to find his voice. He had just been offered everything he'd ever dreamed of. And yet he'd come to this luncheon believing that he'd lost everything that would ever matter to him.

But as he was about to speak Celeste's angry voice had both men turning to her.

''Aren't the two of you putting the horse before the cart? When does a declaration of love become a partnership? How dare you two try to manipulate my life?''

Paddy smiled. ''Darlin' lass, I was just…''

''You've chosen the perfect partner for me? And you think I ought to be grateful?''

''Darlin', I…''

Drew touched a hand to the old man's arm. ''If you're smart, you and Jeremiah will get out of here while you still have your skin.''

''I think…'' Paddy nodded toward his friend, and the two old men started toward the door. ''I'll just leave the two of you alone to work things out now.''

''Oh, no, you don't.'' Celeste started after her grandfather, but Drew caught her by the arm and held her until the two raced out the door, slamming it behind them.

''How can you possibly let him get away with this?'' Celeste's eyes reminded him of the sea just before a storm. ''He has no right trying to meddle in our…''

He kissed her, cutting off her protest. It was the only way he knew to silence her.

When they came up for air she sputtered, ''And furthermore…''

He kissed her again, this time lingering over her lips until the heat began to grow and spread.

''You're right,'' he whispered against her

mouth. "Absolutely right. And I'll tell him so in just a minute."

And then, because he couldn't bear to end it, he simply took the kiss deeper, until they were both gasping for breath.

"But first..." He spoke the words against her mouth, then inside her mouth, unwilling to give up her lips for even a moment. "...I have to tell you something."

"What?" She wrapped her arms around his waist, to anchor herself. She felt just a little weak and lightheaded, and it annoyed her at a time when she needed to be strong and firm.

"I don't just love you, Lessie."

"You don't?" His words seemed to be spinning around in her mind.

"I want more than love. I want that partnership your grandfather spoke of. And I'm not talking about business. I'm talking about life. Wherever we go, however often we pull up stakes and travel on, I want us to be together."

"Oh, Drew. Are you talking about...marriage?"

"You bet I am."

"Do people still do that?"

He merely grinned. "I'm told it's becoming a trend again."

"But how can it work in our case? We'll be constantly traveling."

He nodded. "Constantly."

"And next you'll probably want children."

He paused. "Don't you?"

She shrugged. "Would you like to raise children while moving all around the world?"

He thought for a moment. "I suppose you're right. Look at you."

She drew back to study his face. "What does that mean? My sisters and I had a wonderful, adventurous childhood. I wouldn't trade it for anything. And if I want to drag children around the world with me, I will."

"All right." He kissed the tip of her nose. "If you insist."

She shot him a dark look. "You're manipulating me again."

"Me?" He looked aghast. "I just want what you want. Do you want love? Marriage? Family?"

"I do."

"All right. There you are. So do I. I want the happy ending, Lessie. Don't you believe in forever after?"

"Forever after? I guess I do." She felt her heart turn somersaults in her chest, leaving her feeling dizzy. Right this minute, she needed to hear those words over and over. "Tell me again."

"I love you, Celeste Sullivan. More than anything in the world. Nothing matters except that we're together. Please say you'll marry me."

"Oh, what a lovely proposal. Yes. Oh, yes,

Drew. Yes, I'll marry you. And whether we stay here, or move on, it won't matter, will it?''

''Not a bit. Home is wherever we are, my love.''

Home. It was a word that had never mattered to her before. She was a woman who had traveled the world over and always felt at home. But now, this minute, she realized that she'd just found something better than home. It wasn't a place. It was a feeling. It was here. Here in Drew's arms, she'd finally come home.

And Grandpa Sully had known.

Maybe she'd forgive him. After she made him suffer a bit.

As those warm, firm lips covered hers, and those big, clever hands began to weave their spell, she sighed and gave herself up to the special magic of this man's love. A love that had survived doubt and separation, and the fear of betrayal.

It was, she had no doubt, a love that would survive for all time.

Epilogue

"Oh, my." Lizbeth, dressed in a pink, ankle-skimming gown of raw silk, hurried out to the courtyard just as the last candle was in place. The staff of the Old Liberty Tavern had outdone themselves, turning the inn and its courtyard into a wedding wonderland. There seemed to be acres of white flowers and glossy white candles on the flagstones, on tables, in every corner, as well as yards of white tulle twisted with tiny twinkling lights around every light fixture. "Isn't this just perfect for our Celeste?"

Her older sister, Alex, wearing pale yellow silk, nodded. "Very chic. I don't know how she manages to make even this vintage tavern look upscale.

Next year, it'll probably be featured in every bridal magazine, and she'll have more weddings than she can handle.''

Lizbeth shook her head, sending blond curls dancing. ''Not our Celeste. There is no such thing as more of anything than she can handle. Especially now that she has Drew by her side.'' She smiled dreamily. ''Aren't they a team?''

''Yeah. They're almost too perfect to believe.'' Alex grinned. ''Speaking of teams, we'd better hustle Celeste upstairs and get her ready. Knowing her, she's probably still in her office giving last-minute orders to the staff.''

The two sisters were laughing minutes later when they dragged Celeste out of her office and into the elevator. All the way up, she continued talking on the phone, booking a party for the following month.

''That's it.'' At the door Alex removed the phone from her sister's hand and set it on a table. ''If it rings again, you're going to ignore it.''

''But it could be…''

''I don't care if it's the queen of England. She's going to have to wait until after your wedding to book her party.''

Laughing, the two sisters dragged their youngest sister to the shower, then helped her with her makeup, and finally into her gown, which bore the label of one of the finest fashion designers in Paris.

Then they stood back to admire and had to fight the tears that threatened.

The gown suited her to perfection. Sophisticated and unadorned. A long straight column of white silk, with a rounded neckline that fell just off the shoulders, and long, narrow sleeves. Her wonderful red hair fell soft and loose beneath a veil anchored by a tiny crown of pearls.

"Oh, Celeste." Lizbeth blinked hard to keep from embarrassing herself. "You look so beautiful."

"You belong on the cover of a magazine." Alex grinned. "You'll certainly fit right in with that elegant setting downstairs." She shook her head. "Not that I had a moment's doubt that your wedding would be anything but the grandest event of the year."

The three young women looked up at a knock on the door. Their parents entered, followed by the rest of the family. Alex's husband, Grant, and Lizbeth's husband, Colin, as well as Patrick Sullivan gathered around the bride for hugs and kisses.

While her mother was forced to wipe away tears, her father gathered her close for a kiss. And all the while Patrick Sullivan stood to one side, watching with pride.

Jeremiah Cross poked his head through the open door. "The minister is downstairs, waiting for the happy couple. And the staff has begun seating the guests.''

He diplomatically ushered everyone from the room, leaving Celeste alone with her grandfather.

He stood looking at her with such pride gleaming in those blue eyes. ''Am I forgiven yet, darlin' lass?''

She nodded. ''How could I stay angry with you, Grandpa Sully? I guess you just couldn't help meddling, since you know us so well.''

''Ah. That I do.'' He smiled. ''Living in hotels for a lifetime has affected all of us differently. Your sister, Alex, had a need to break away from the throngs of people, both staff and guests, to find herself in the quiet of nature. Lizbeth, on the other hand, had a desperate need for a home of her own. And then there's you, darlin' Celeste. You're a corporate animal, and what you've always needed was a man who understood that drive, and shared it, the way your grandmother shared my life, and your parents share their love of the business. I believe you've found the perfect soul mate in Andrew.'' He kissed her cheek and started toward the door. ''Which reminds me, Jeremiah reported that your perfect mate is about as restless as a tiger on a leash. I think I'll pay him a quick visit before he starts down that aisle. I'll see if I can calm the beast.''

He walked across the hall and knocked. At a call

from within, Patrick Sullivan opened the door and stepped inside. Drew turned from the balcony, where he'd been pacing, watching the crowd below.

Seeing the frown line between his brows, the old man paused. "Having second thoughts, Andrew?"

Drew shook his head. "Not about marrying Celeste. But I've been standing here thinking about the circumstances that brought me here."

The old man started to back away. "Maybe you ought to go see your bride-to-be. She's in need of your calming influence, lad."

"You'd like that, wouldn't you? Especially since seeing Celeste would muddle all my brain cells and prevent me from thinking what I've just been thinking."

"What do you mean by that?" Patrick gave a nervous smile.

Drew advanced on him. "I mean I've had time to sort all this out, and I've come to the conclusion that you're a conniving old…" He shook his head. "If I hadn't been so blinded by love, I'd have figured this out a whole lot sooner."

"I don't know what you…"

"Oh, yes, you do. You, along with your very good friend Jeremiah, orchestrated this entire thing from beginning to end. It was you who sent that profit-and-loss sheet to Van Dorn in the first place, wasn't it? You who planted the seed in the minds of the board of directors of Van Dorn Hotels, knowing they'd send me here to look into buying it for them. You who kept me here with one excuse after another, until your granddaughter and I couldn't resist each other any longer. Why?''

The old man merely smiled. ''The two of you didn't make it easy. In fact, Jeremiah and I were running out of excuses. He'd phone me, complaining that he kept throwing you together, and one thing or another would keep you apart. We were almost ready to give up.''

Before Drew could say a word he held up a hand. ''Did you think I didn't see the way you two suffered when you went your separate ways?''

''It was our pain. Our business.''

''Oh, to be sure. But Celeste's business has always been mine. I saw the way she threw herself into her work with even more determination than before. And I kept track of your career as well. I knew why you'd climbed the corporate ladder so quickly at Van Dorn. It was talent and hard work. Something you and my darlin' Celeste have in abundance. There you were, both of you trying so hard to heal your broken hearts. And I thought, since it was my fault you left, it was up to me to bring you back.''

''But why me, Paddy?'' Drew stared into the old man's eyes, searching for answers. ''Why were you so determined that I was the right one for your granddaughter?''

"That's easy. The first time I saw you, putting yourself through college by working harder than anyone else, by taking all the shifts nobody else was willing to take, I knew you, Andrew."

"I don't understand. You knew me?"

"As well as I know myself." The old man clapped a hand on Drew's shoulder. "I saw an ambitious, driven young man, determined to get ahead on his own. Determined to convince himself and the woman he loved, a woman who came from money and privilege, that he was worthy of that love." He chuckled. "Don't you see, lad? I knew you because you were me, Andrew. I saw myself in you. And I understood that you needed to find out in your own way. And so I let you go, knowing it was breaking the hearts of the two people who meant everything in the world to me."

"But why now? What made you orchestrate this little deal now?"

"The time was right. You've proven yourself at Van Dorn. If I waited much longer, you'd be ascending the presidency there instead of where you belong. And I was afraid Celeste might start to get the itch to move on, and I'd be facing another missed opportunity. This was the right place, the right time. And I knew I had to move on it before

it slipped by me. By us all.'' He stuck out his hand.
''Am I forgiven?''

''That depends.'' Drew bit back the smile that
threatened and stared at the outstretched hand.
''Just what is it you're offering me?''

''The presidency. Though you'll have to share
it with a certain fiery young bride. Deal?''

Drew grinned. ''Deal.'' He caught the old man's
hand in his, then drew him close for a hug. ''I'd
come back even without the offer of an executive
position.''

''I know that, lad.''

''You've always been the father I never had,
Paddy.''

''And you're the grandson I never had, Andrew.
And I hope you'll keep this little conversation between the two of us, for at least fifty years or so.''
The old man stepped back. ''Now, you'd better go
to your bride. The crowd down there is probably
getting restless.''

The two men walked to the door and stepped
out into the hall.

As he started toward the elevator Paddy Sullivan
paused. ''By the way, I spoke with Eric Van Dorn.
He told me you were the most promising employee
he'd ever hooked. He told me he probably didn't
play that one right. He let you slip off the line.''

''He's wrong, Paddy. I wiggled off. All by my-

self.'' Drew paused. "With a little help from you
and Jeremiah.''

He was still grinning as he watched the old man
stride away. He crossed the hall and knocked on
Celeste's door, then stepped inside.

She turned from the balcony to face him, and he
felt all the breath leave his lungs.

She started toward him and paused to pick up
the elegant nosegay of white roses and ivy from a
nearby table. "I love the flowers, Drew. Lizbeth
told me you went to the town market early this
morning to pick them out yourself.''

He nodded.

"What's wrong?" Alarmed, she walked closer
and reached out a hand to him, but he surprised
her by drawing back.

"Wait a minute." He held up a hand. "I want
to look at you a minute more.''

His smile was slow to come, but when it did,
she felt her heart begin to settle.

"You're so beautiful, you take my breath
away.''

"You're not bad yourself." She studied the way
he looked in black tie. "Maybe Sullivan Hotels
should use you in their next advertising cam-
paign.''

He laughed and stepped closer to brush a kiss
over her lips. "There's the woman I know. Always

thinking about business, even on her wedding day.''

''And what about you? Tell the truth. Haven't you been thinking that this is the perfect setting for weddings?''

He nodded. ''In fact, I've been wondering if we ought to look into buying the property next door to that little cottage. We could add a dance pavilion, and maybe attract summer concerts.''

He saw the excitement in her eyes and gave a roar of laughter. ''You see? It's contagious. I can see that in a few years we won't even have to speak. One of us will have a thought and the other will simply pick up on it.'' He drew her into his arms and pressed his mouth to her temple. ''In fact, I'll bet you can read my mind right now. Let's try it.''

She brought her hand to his cheek and stared into those gray mysterious depths. ''Umm. Yes. I like the way you think, Mr. Hampton. But I do think we'd better wait a while for that. At least until after we've spoken our vows and dispensed with our guests.''

He caught her hand. ''Then let's get started. I can't wait to spend the rest of my life with you.''

As they walked to the elevator and stepped inside, they turned to each other with matching looks of love.

Downstairs they walked past the line of employees who smiled and waved as they made their way to the courtyard. Daniel O'Malley looked handsome in his formal wear. Bitsy Hillerman was wiping a tear from her eye. Jeremiah stood guard at the entrance to the courtyard.

Celeste paused to press a kiss to his weathered cheek. "You look as happy about this as Grandpa Sully."

The old man leaned close to whisper, "Happier, if truth be told. I do like your Mr. Hampton."

"Then do you suppose you might be able to start calling him Drew?"

The old man thought a moment, then nodded. "I suppose, as long as he's now part of the family."

He turned to Drew and offered his handshake. "Congratulations, Drew. You're a lucky man indeed."

"Thank you, Jeremiah."

As they stepped out into the courtyard and started toward the waiting minister, Drew leaned close to whisper, "He's right, you know. I am a lucky man. And on our fiftieth wedding anniversary, I'll have quite a tale to share with you."

"Really?" Celeste looked over to see her family. Her father and mother, holding hands and looking as much in love as they had when she was a little girl. Her sisters, now happily married, stand-

ing proudly beside their husbands. And her be-
loved Grandpa Sully, beaming with such pride.

And then she turned to Drew and everyone else
faded from sight. It occurred to her that, though
nothing had changed in her life, everything had
changed. She still didn't know where she'd be a
year from now. What country she'd call home. Or
even what continent. But as long as she had this
man beside her, she would always be home.

"I love you, Drew Hampton."

"Not nearly as much as I love you, Celeste Sullivan." He looked down at her and gave her one
of those heart-stopping grins, and she knew that
she had found her perfect life partner. He would
feed her when she forgot to eat. Shelter her when
she found herself in a storm. And would share not
only her love, but her dreams as well.

They were, she knew without a doubt, a perfect
fit. Partners. Forever.

* * * * *

Silhouette®

INTIMATE MOMENTS™

presents a riveting 12-book continuity series:

a Year of loving dangerously

Where passion rules and nothing is what it seems...

When dishonor threatens a top-secret agency, the brave men and women of SPEAR are prepared to risk it all as they put their lives—and their hearts—on the line.

Available April 2001:

THE WAY WE WED
by Pat Warren

They had married in secret, two undercover agents with nothing to lose—except maybe the love of a lifetime. For though Jeff Kirby tried to keep Tish Buckner by his side, tragedy tore the newlyweds apart. Now Tish's life hung in the balance, and Jeff was hoping against hope that he and Tish would get a second chance at the life they'd once dreamed of. For this time, the determined M.D. wouldn't let his woman get away!

July 2000: MISSION: IRRESISTIBLE by Sharon Sala #1016
August: UNDERCOVER BRIDE by Kylie Brant #1022
September: NIGHT OF NO RETURN by Eileen Wilks #1028
October: HER SECRET WEAPON by Beverly Barton #1034
November: HERO AT LARGE by Robyn Amos #1040
December: STRANGERS WHEN WE MARRIED by Carla Cassidy #1046
January 2001: THE SPY WHO LOVED HIM by Merline Lovelace #1052
February: SOMEONE TO WATCH OVER HER by Margaret Watson #1058
March: THE ENEMY'S DAUGHTER by Linda Turner #1064
April: THE WAY WE WED by Pat Warren #1070
May: CINDERELLA'S SECRET AGENT by Ingrid Weaver #1076
June: FAMILIAR STRANGER by Sharon Sala #1082

*Available only from Silhouette Intimate Moments
at your favorite retail outlet.*

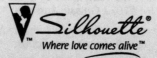
Silhouette®

Where love comes alive™

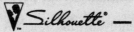

LINDSAY McKENNA

continues her most popular series with a
brand-new, longer-length book.

And it's the story you've been waiting for....

Morgan's Mercenaries:
Heart of Stone

They had met before. Battled before. And
Captain Maya Stevenson had never again
wanted to lay eyes on Major Dane York—
the man who once tried to destroy
her military career! But on their latest
mission together, Maya discovered that beneath
the fury in Dane's eyes lay a raging passion. Now she
struggled against dangerous desire, as Dane's command
over her seemed greater still. For this time, he laid claim
to her heart....

Only from Lindsay McKenna and Silhouette Books!

"When it comes to action and romance,
nobody does it better than Ms. McKenna."
—*Romantic Times Magazine*

Available in March at your favorite retail outlet.

Silhouette®
Where love comes alive™

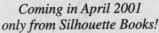